The Meerkat Wars

Vita Vya Meerkat

H. S. Toshack

Illustrations by Nelson McAlister

Other books in the series:
Paka Mdogo
The Gradual Elephant

First published in North America
by
PakaMdogo Press 2012

The moral right of the author has been asserted
A CIP record of this book is available from the British Library

ISBN 978-0-9563236-2-0

A set of free, downloadable teaching resources (structured in line with the **UK National Literacy Strategies** and tied in to the **US Common Core State Standards**, but designed to help all young readers explore the text fully, and extend their enjoyment of it) is available in the Children's section of the LitWorks.com website.
. **Go to http://www.litworks.com/childrens.php**

Sheena the little black-and-white cat has made her third secret trip to **Baragandiri National Park.** She is just as curious as she was before; and this time she travels further into the Park, and much further into the lives of some of the animals who live in it.

She makes friends with the **Duwara**, a tribe of Meerkats; and if you are friends with someone you need to help them when they are in trouble. When they're in Big Trouble (fighting a war) you may have to help them a Lot.

But helping them doesn't necessarily mean helping them to win...

The map on Pages 2 and 3 will show you a new part of **Baragandiri**; and the story will perhaps tell you some new things about how animals (and people) behave.

To Sheena...
...and with many thanks once more to Janet

Contents

Chapter One: Kisusuli

If you say no to my question
You will leave here safe and sound;
But if your answer is yes
You may die writhing on the ground.

She was already thirsty. It was still quite early in the morning, and she was already thirsty. So when she found the insect underneath the fallen tree-trunk, she immediately began to consider how juicy it might be. When you're very thirsty, liquids other than water can make you feel better, even if they're a bit sticky or slimy.

'How juicy are you, little insect?' she asked out loud. She didn't expect the insect to reply. She was talking to herself. She blamed the hot African sun, which was making her light-headed.

She hadn't realised how different things would be this time.

The day before, Sheena the family cat had happily jumped up into the back of *Great White,* the family Land Rover, when no-one was looking, and hidden among the boxes and bags. The Allens were bustling around doing last-minute things before setting off on safari once more; and they kept adding more boxes and bags, tools and tent-bits to those already in the Land Rover. They piled them in on top of the ones Sheena had squeezed down among, so that she felt extra squashed but extra out of sight.

The family hadn't been so well organised this time. They'd decided to drive North at the last minute, when a very different

1

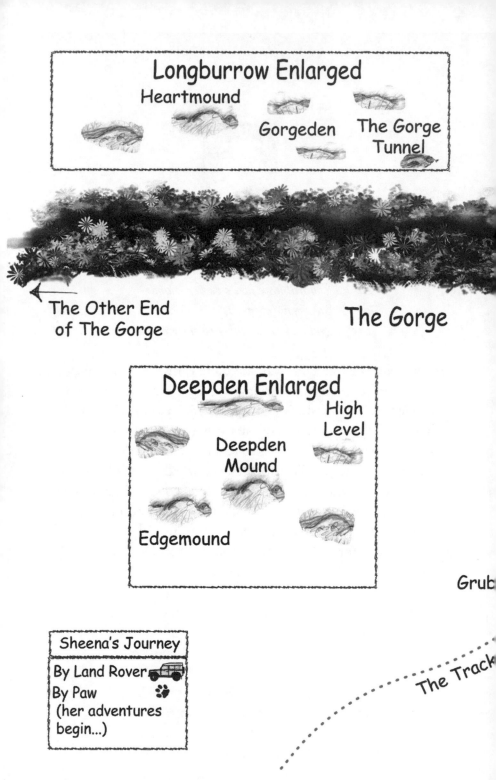

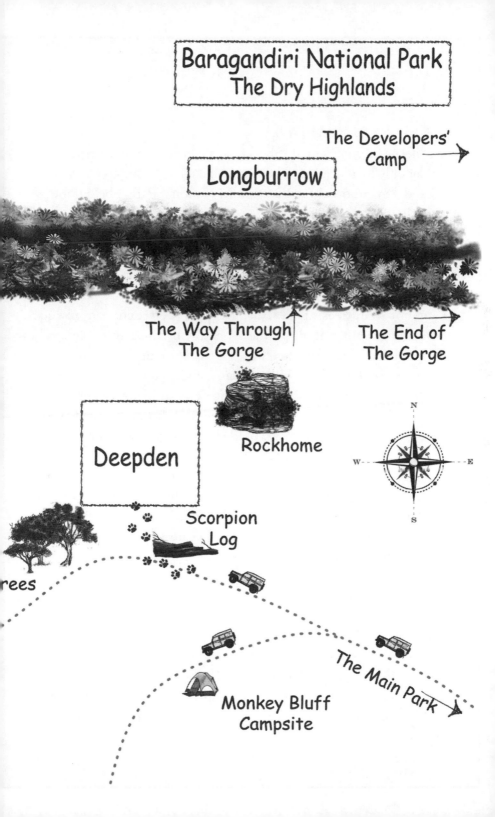

holiday plan had gone wrong.

Sheena was delighted. She couldn't have sneaked aboard an airplane flying to the Seychelles, but she could easily creep aboard a Land Rover bound for Baragandiri National Park. She'd done it twice before, after all.

This was not the Park as she remembered it, however. When the Allens had come on safari previously, they had camped down in the river valley, where there was green grass, and water both running (in rivers) and still (in pools), and even fruit (strange) on some of the trees. Dad Allen, in his determination to do Something Different this time – partly because they were all disappointed about the Seychelles – had decided to drive right through to the other side of Baragandiri, up onto The Dry Highlands. Amy couldn't quite get it right and kept calling them The High Drylands. When he found out how hot they were during the daytime, Thomas would call them the Deep Frylands.

Now Sheena herself had been left high and dry.

The family had set up camp in the shade of a large tree, at a place Mum Allen, reading from the map they had been given at the Park Gate, said was called Monkey Bluff. They were planning to stay for ten whole days this time, because that was how long they'd intended to go to the Seychelles for; and they'd brought lots of extra water and other supplies (hence the squeeze Sheena had found herself in).

Other people before them had camped under the same tree and used up all the dead wood nearby. Dad Allen had driven off to find more so that they could have a cheery fire when darkness fell and it got cold (which it did up here at night, no matter how hot it was during the day). Sheena had gone with him...unknown to him, of course, since her presence was unknown to them all and she was supposed to be safely tucked up back home fat

4

chance. She was here for more fat adventures.

She'd got a big fat shock, however, when Dad Allen climbed back into the Land Rover without warning and drove off back towards the campsite in a cloud of dust, leaving her behind under the low bush she'd nosily wriggled into. The dust swirled in amongst the leaves and made her sneeze; but it was a very dry sneeze, since she had hardly any moisture to spare.

She had no idea why he'd gone off in such a hurry: he'd picked up hardly any wood. Perhaps it had something to do with the slight hissing noise she'd heard coming from one of the rear tyres.

'You'll never know how juicy.'

The insect *had* answered her; and its voice was high and dry too, and rather creaky and scratchy.

'Answer my question.'

This was not Sheena demanding a reply, but the insect, still speaking creakily (and cheekily, Sheena thought. What question, anyway? It hadn't asked one.) As it spoke it crawled out from under the tree-trunk. It was bigger than Sheena had realised; and it was obviously not afraid of her.

It was a strange looking creature, like a miniature black lobster. (Sheena came originally from the Caribbean, as you may already know, and she remembered full well what lobsters looked like and how good their tails tasted.) Its tail was longer and thinner than a lobster's, however; and it had claws, unlike Caribbean lobsters at least, and it was waving them at Sheena as it spoke. Sheena began to suspect what it was.

'What question?' asked Sheena.

She knew that when someone asks you a question, they are also telling you something, whether they realise it or not. 'How long are you going shopping for, Mum?' from Thomas usually meant, 'I've got a plan.' When Amy asked, 'Whose is this chocolate biscuit?' she was saying, 'I'm going to eat this chocolate biscuit unless you speak very quickly.' So Sheena was interested in what this creature's question was.

'*This* question,' it said. The back part of its body suddenly arched upwards and forwards, and its long tail sprang up over its head and hung there like a question mark. Then Sheena knew what the creature was; and she instantly lost interest in the matter of its juiciness. It was a scorpion.

'But you have to tell me what the question means,' said Sheena, 'otherwise I'm likely to get the answer wrong.'

As things stood, the question could be anything from *Don't you think my tail is beautiful?* to *What's the weather like where you come from?*

This was not a friendly creature, however. Its whole body was bristling with suspicion, including the short black hairs on its legs. Sheena also noticed how sharp the end of its tail was. It didn't just come to a point: the tip was shaped like a bulbous rose-thorn, and was clearly meant for stabbing.

'The question *means*,' said the scorpion, 'Do you *mean* me any *harm*?'

Its tail curved further forward, threateningly, and Sheena saw a glistening at the tip, as if a small drop of liquid was forming there. Then there was a hissing sound, much sharper than the one that had come from the Land Rover's tyre – another warning, beyond doubt.

Now Sheena had been here before. Well, not *here*, exactly, in this place, and not *here*, exactly, with a creature like this, but *here*, in a similar situation. The last time had been down by a dry river bed in a very different part of the Park, and the creature had been a swila, a cobra, who after hissing at her had spat in her eyes and blinded her very painfully. So she took a step back.

6

'Yes, I can squirt my poison at you,' said the scorpion, 'and I can sting you, and if I do you'll squirm in the dust and die. So answer my question.'

'Why would I mean you any harm?' Sheena asked.

This was answering a question with a question, which could be very irritating, she knew. She could instead have answered a hiss with a hiss; but she didn't have a sting, and couldn't squirt poison, so she proceeded cautiously.

'Because you have teeth. Teeth mean trouble.'

'Hisses means trouble as well. How did you do that? You're not a snake.'

Sheena was trying hard to turn a challenge into a conversation.

'I rub my jaws together, like this.'

The scorpion repeated his warning noise, and Sheena took one more step back. She had decided to maintain a respectful hisstance: the last thing she wanted was for the question mark to become a puncturation mark.

'I wouldn't have thought you would need to worry too much about teeth. Scorpions pack a pretty powerful punch.'

She knew about scorpions since Thomas knew about scorpions and Sheena knew much of what Thomas knew.

'What does that mean, *pack a pretty powerful punch*?' asked the scorpion.

Sheena tried a more appropriate phrase. 'I should have said *stock a simply stunning sting*.

'What animals are you afraid of, in particular?' she continued.

'Animals like you, that take an interest in us. Animals that think juicy.'

('That's all animals,' Sheena thought to herself.)

'It's not just animals, it's centipedes, snakes, tarantulas, lizards and birds. They'd all eat us if we weren't on our guard.'

7

'What do *you* eat?'

'Oh, small animals, centipedes, snakes, tarantulas, lizards and little birds.'

('Fair dos, then,' Sheena thought again.)

'It's all a question of who gets his sting in first, or his bite, or his peck.'

('What happened to scratch?' Sheena thought. That was what she was good at.)

'You don't look big enough to kill a bird,' she said.

'Well, not me personally, of course. But I've got some cousins who are nearly as big as you are. When we first of all came out of the sea forty million years ago we were a metre long.'

Sheena had been surprised before by how much so-called wild (i.e. apparently uneducated) creatures knew about their own history, and how proud they usually were of it.

'Think about that!'

Sheena thought about it, and didn't like the idea. Thomas had a model Scorpion tank. He would have thought a Scorpion tank armed with a Stinger missile was an interesting item of warfare hardware.

She had just about decided to walk away from this encounter, since it clearly wasn't going to be thirst-quenching, when there was a rustling in the bushes next to the log. A sharp nose poked out between the leaves, then a narrow face, and suddenly an animal roughly her own shape but quite a lot smaller than she was bounded out into the open. Its tail, covered in short hair, was very long, and stuck straight up in the air.

The scorpion tried to scuttle back under the log, but was not quick enough. The new arrival pounced forwards and bit down on the scorpion's tail with a cracking noise. Forty million years of history don't count for much when it comes to the crunch.

The attacker's tactic was plain: bite the bit that could do the damage, and immobilise it.

Something went very wrong, however. He had taken hold too close to the scorpion's body and there was enough tail protruding from the side of his mouth to curve round so that the stinging thorn, now dripping with poison, went into his cheek.

'Ow!' he said.

Chapter Two: Suricate

My family name is part Christmas bird,
But instead of feathers I have fur.
My special name sounds feline,
But I growl and chirp, I don't purr.

'Ow! Ow! That hurts!'

The animal had let go of the scorpion and jumped backwards. The scorpion quickly scuttled off under the tree-trunk, its broken tail dragging in the dust.

'It's not supposed to hurt like that!' said the animal, complainingly. Its tail suddenly looked less strong, lost some of its straightness, then began to droop towards the ground.

'You're not supposed to get stung like that. You were careless.'

This comment came from inside the bush. Another animal, similar to the first in shape but quite a bit larger, stepped out from among the leaves.

'And you couldn't have picked a worse Kisusuli to be careless with. That was a Black Hairy Thick-Tail. You should have waited for me. I'd have told you to leave it alone. You aren't ready for those, yet, Pebble.'

It sounded as if Pebble was doing some sort of training – dangerous training.

'I hope you aren't going to have a problem, now. Black Hairy Thick-Tail venom is very powerful, and very quick-acting.'

'But I thought we were immune, Sandstepper. That's what it said in the lesson.'

'You obviously weren't listening closely enough. Crossclaw said we're immune *up to a point*. We don't suffer as badly as other animals; but you aren't fully grown yet; and it's the first time you've been stung; and it was a very bad scorpion to tangle with, as I've said; and it stung you in a very bad place. So tell me if you begin to feel funny.'

'I feel sore is what I feel; and *that's* not funny.'

They ignored Sheena while they spoke, and she was able to look them over thoroughly. The larger one was about her size but more slender. Both animals' fur was mid-brown in colour, and they had darker brown bars across their backs.

The one who had been stung was crouching on the ground, but the second one had now stood up on his hind legs as if this

11

were quite natural to him. His short front legs were tucked in against his chest and he was holding his paws together in front of his round little stomach. His claws were big but blunt. His neck was long and thin, and his head, also long and thin, sat on it at right-angles like the carved handle of a walking-stick. The top of his head was flat, and the fur on it was short and even, so that he looked as if he had had a very close military crew-cut.

His face was pointed, and his light brown eyes, set in circles of black fur, were bright and piercing. His ears, small, dark and rounded, were in keeping with the streamlined appearance of his head. Altogether he looked a sharp little animal. He was also rather elegant.

Sheena thought they were both probably mongooses.

The larger animal spoke again.

'Don't rub your cheek like that. You'll just spread the poison.'

Pebble had been licking a front paw and trying to clean his wound with it – very much what Sheena would have done if she'd been injured like that.

'I've got a bitter taste in my mouth. I think the sting went right through my cheek.'

('If that's the case he'll be able to lick his wound from inside,' thought Sheena. 'Very convenient.')

'Will it matter if some of the poison goes down my throat?'

'No, you'll just digest it. It's the poison that gets into your blood that may harm you.'

'How will I know?'

Their voices were quite high-pitched and they had been talking quickly. The animal called Sandstepper now began to speak more slowly, heavily and distantly, as if he were delivering a lecture.

'Symptoms of scorpion envenomation:

'1. Intense pain at the sting site, beginning immediately.'

'Got that,' said Pebble. 'Ow!'

'2. Burning sensations elsewhere in the body.'

'Getting that. Ow!'

'3. Paraesthesia – an abnormal sensitivity, with pins and needles in the paws, face and scalp.'

'I feel it! I feel it! I'm tingling!'

'4. Excessive salivation.'

Pebble now began to drool, and saliva dripped into the dust from the end of his pointed mouth.

It was all happening very *pat* – on cue; and Sheena began to suspect that this might be less scorpion-poison than self-persuasion. Pebble was just imagining he was experiencing the symptoms on Sandstepper's list.

'5. Dysarthria – difficulty in talking.'

'Whatth...goin...tappen...tme? My...gwin...die?'

'6. Restlessness and anxiety.'

Pebble now stood up. He wasn't nearly as tall as his companion. He began to walk in circles, faster and faster.

'7. Ataxia – a lack of muscle coordination, involuntary movements, tremors and muscle weakness.'

Pebble started to stagger. Then his feet got tangled, his knees gave way and he collapsed in a twitching heap in the centre of the circle he had made in the dust.

'8. Ptosis – patient has droopy eyelids.'

Pebble's eyelids were indeed beginning to droop...but then so were Sheena's, almost: this was a long lecture, with lots of difficult words in it.

'9. Nausea and vomiting.

'10. Diarrhoea.'

Sheena decided it was probably time to leave.

'11. No you can't leave. We need your help.'

For the first time Sandstepper turned towards Sheena. It now became apparent that the lecture had been delivered in part to her so that she would know what was going on.

'12. Soon he'll have Dyspnoea – difficulty in breathing, and then he won't be able to breathe at all, and then he'll die. We need to get him back to Deepden, quickly. The Ndugu may be able to save him.

'You've got a broad back, and strong legs. You look like you're made for carrying. You can carry him.'

There was an assumption in his words that Sheena found strange, a belief that she would carry just because she could, and that she would help simply because help was needed.

Sheena wasn't used to carrying, no matter how strong her legs looked; but she was very used to carrying *on* (something awful) when she was taken for granted, like when it was wrongly assumed that she wanted to be inside the house when she wanted to be out, or that she would sit on a knee simply because she had been placed there.

She looked again at Pebble, now twisting in pain on the ground with saliva trickling from one corner of his mouth. She realised two things. Firstly, these were not imaginary symptoms: Pebble was dying. Secondly, she would help.

She backed towards the injured meerkat and crouched down, pushing her rump against him. Sandstepper nudged, nosed, persuaded Pebble onto his feet. Pebble tottered on the spot for a moment, spun once, then flopped forward over Sheena's back, his front legs hanging down on either side of her shoulders. She straightened her legs, slowly. He started to slide off backwards. She flattened her spine. Then she moved backwards against the tree-trunk and used it to push the limp body further up towards her head.

When she stepped forward again, cautiously, Pebble stayed in place. Sandstepper set off, on all fours. Sheena followed.

Pebble had stopped twitching, and seemed to be unconscious. She could feel his cold dribble on the back of her neck.

'Hope he doesn't get to Symptoms Numbers 9 and 10 anytime soon,' she thought.

Sandstepper led her past the bush he and Pebble had emerged from. The ground ahead was open, and flat, and dry-looking. Heat wavered above it. Sheena remembered how thirsty she was.

Pebble was heavy but not terribly heavy, and she had no difficulty carrying him to begin with. After a while, however, the ground became sandier and softer, and the extra weight on her back meant that her paws sank deeply into it. What had begun as a walk became a trudge. She was afraid that before long it would become a wade.

Sandstepper, in contrast, moved over the soft ground easily, and that wasn't just because he wasn't carrying another one of him. His rear paws were large for his size; and his front ones, although they had seemed narrow when they hung downwards, spread out when he placed them on the ground.

'In addition,' said Sandstepper, who had done a bit of talking as they travelled (to jolly her along, Sheena suspected), 'the skin between my claws has grown more than usual, and I'm more than usually good at walking on sand. Hence my name.'

The fact that Sandstepper had webbed feet didn't help Sheena much. She was tiring.

Then they rounded a small grove of trees, and she saw that the ground ahead rose towards a higher level. There was more green on the surface up there – not grass, but something like it; and she knew that would make for easier walking. They would need to climb a little to reach it, however. So she stopped at the last tree and leant back against it to push Pebble further up towards her shoulders. He was still wholly unconscious, and still dribbling, but at least she could feel him breathing.

They set off up the gradient. Fortunately it was not so steep as to cause Pebble to slide down towards her tail.

As they climbed she began to experience some scorpion envenomation symptoms herself, even though she had not been stung.

5. Dysarthria: She now had difficulty answering Sandstepper when he asked (as he had done repeatedly since they set off), 'Are you alright?' When she tried to speak, her head started spinning. She could have added a new symptom to the list – *Dizzyarthria.*

7. Ataxia: Her legs were increasingly wobbly, and she suffered several ataxias of stumbling.

12. Dyspnoea: She was thoroughly out of breath by the time they were half-way up the slope. She felt another new symptom – *Collapsnear.*

She wished she could experience a bit of *4. Excessive salivation;* but her mouth was dry, dry.

Sandstepper noticed she was having difficulty.

'Don't worry, it isn't far. We never hunt a long way from our burrow.'

Once they had reached the top of the slope Sheena slowed down to regain her breath. The ground was firmer, as she thought it would be, and the going indeed easier. The green ground cover did not stretch on uninterrupted, however: it was broken up by wide sandy patches. Several of the patches had large mounds in the centre. On top of the largest mound stood a thin, upright figure, with a pointed head and face, looking straight at them. It was the same kind of animal as Sandstepper and Pebble. It barked, once, sharply.

The mound of sand exploded. Eight or ten similar animals burst out from its sides and jumped up alongside the first one, standing in exactly the same posture, sharp snouts towards the newcomers, front paws resting on their stomachs. From here they looked identical; and they began to behave identically. They scratched backwards, violently, with their clawed hind feet, digging into the surface of the mound so that clouds of dust rose in the air, partly hiding them. Then they started jumping up and down and snarling ferociously.

The effect of the dust and the jumping and the snarling was startling. The whole group looked to be pounding forwards,

17

down from the mound and across the earth, ready to attack. They would be here in a flash.

Then Sheena realised they wouldn't be here at all. They hadn't moved from the top of the mound. It was all an illusion, created by the animals so that they could frighten off intruders without having to move away from their burrow entrance.

'I'd better go ahead. You wait here,' said Sandstepper, and he walked forward, slowly.

Sheena didn't do what she was told (not for the first time in her life). Pebble was no longer a pebble, he was a heavy rock, and she knew that if she didn't get him off her back soon her legs would buckle under her and he would slide off into the sand anyway, well short of where he needed to be. There was no way she would be able to get him back on to carry him the rest of the way; and there was no guaranteeing that these other funny animals, for all their vigorous jumping up and down, would be able to carry him themselves. If he needed to be taken down into the burrow (which she imagined would be something like a rabbit warren) then she would have to do it. So she couldn't put him down, and she couldn't risk stopping; she therefore kept going, following a few feet behind Sandstepper and staggering slightly.

This threw the jumping animals into a frenzy.

'Stop! We know who you are! Who are you? We know what you want! What do you want? Stay there! Go away!'

Their shouting was confused, more noise than anything. It was as if they hadn't recognised Sandstepper. Had he brought them to the wrong burrow? Were they going to be attacked?

'It's me – Sandstepper.'

The animals stopped jumping and began to do something else strange. Their heads bobbed up and down, and they peered closely at Sandstepper as he continued to walk steadily forward.

When he reached the foot of the mound he halted. Suddenly one of the animals leaped down in front of him and bounced straight back up again as if he'd landed on a trampoline. In the instant between down and up he took a deep sniff.

His return to the top of the mound touched off another individual, who also leapt, sniff-bounced, then landed back among the group…then another, until it seemed they'd all had a go.

Sheena learnt later that these animals could see very clearly over long distances, but had poor eyesight for near things. That was why they bobbed their heads up and down so much, to get a clearer view of what they were looking at, and a better idea of how far away it was.

They also had a very keen sense of smell and could recognise each other easily, but a very poor smell-memory, so that a member of the group who had been away for just a few hours could not count on being recognised when he returned, and ran the risk of being savaged.

The situation was complicated now by her own smell, and by the strange sight she presented.

'Ah, yes. You could be Sandstepper. You smell a bit like him. But what's that other creature behind you, the one with two heads?'

It was the animal in the centre of the group who spoke. He may have been the biggest of them, but it was hard to tell since he was also standing on the highest point of the mound. He had a slightly darker head than the rest, and there was a little spike of hair towards the back of his skull, as if whoever had given him his crew-cut had missed a bit.

'Half of it's Pebble. He's been Kisusuli-stung. The bottom half's a sort of little cat. She's helped us.

'We need to get Pebble into the burrow quickly. He needs to cool down. The Ndugu may be able to save him.'

Angular heads on long necks turned towards each other, then back towards Sandstepper. The whole group now jumped down from the mound and ran around Sheena, sniffing both her and Pebble. Then a gap opened up in front of her, and she could see a tunnel entrance at the base of the mound. She walked towards it, since that's what she assumed was wanted; but it was immediately obvious that two into one wouldn't go: the tunnel wasn't high enough for her to enter with Pebble on her back.

'Sorry, this is as far as I can take him,' she said, mainly to Sandstepper. She lowered her rear end and straightened her front legs. Pebble slid slowly down her back, rolled over sideways and flopped onto the sand. The other animals gathered around him, and their shadows created some shade over his inert body.

Then he stirred.

'Whyshi…dar?...My…dedyet?'

'*Dysarthria*,' Sheena thought. She had remembered Sandstepper's lecture quite well.

Then Pebble suddenly developed Symptom Number 9, and the animals in the circle took half a step back.

Soon, however, they were able help the injured animal up onto his wobbly legs, and two of them supported him as he moved unsteadily towards the tunnel entrance. As he passed Sheena he seemed to recognise her, and appeared to have some idea of how he had got there.

'Shank…ou,' he said.

The tunnel sloped away into the depths of the mound, and the trio disappeared one by one into the darkness.

As soon as they had done that, most of the other animals ran round to the sides of the mound. There were tunnel entrances there, too, and the animals skittered down them. Only the tall, dark-headed one stayed behind with Sheena and Sandstepper. He was looking closely at Sheena.

Sheena was curious about the tunnel.

'Can I look inside a little way?' she asked. She'd never been in a burrow before. She moved towards the entrance.

The taller animal immediately jumped in front of her. He looked ready to do his dance again.

'It's alright, Tuft,' said Sandstepper.

'But do you trust her?'

'Yes, I do. She saved Pebble. She didn't have to help.'

Tuft stepped aside, reluctantly. Sheena got the impression he was a higher-ranking animal than Sandstepper. He was also more suspicious.

'That's alright. Suspicious is good around here,' she thought to herself.

She put her head into the main tunnel, the one Pebble had gone down. The opening itself, although low, was quite wide. She took a step inside. There was a slightly damp smell, and a lived-in-by-animals smell, and a died-in-by-animals smell, and a time-you-changed-your-socks smell which reminded her of Thomas and made her feel a bit home-sick.

The tunnel branched almost immediately. To the left another tunnel went off at the same level. The main tunnel carried on downwards into the darkness. On the right there was a half-open chamber with things scattered on the floor. She stepped cautiously in. There were old leaves and grass, egg-shells and snail-shells (all broken), a small skull, some tufts of fur, and something she recognised with a little frightened start – a very large scorpion, facing towards her, with its curved and jointed tail hanging menacingly in the air above it.

Sandstepper, looking past her, saw what had made her jump.

'Don't worry! It's dead. It's a demonstration specimen. We use it to show youngsters how to take hold of scorpions, even big ones, without being stung. It seems we need to give them more practice at that.'

Sheena moved further into the main tunnel. The light dimmed, since she was blocking most of it. The tunnel began to narrow, and soon it was only just wide enough for her to move along. Her whiskers were brushing the walls on either side.

Cats are Claustrophobic. They hate being in confined spaces that they think they may not be able to get out of. There was nowhere here for Sheena to turn around, and it seemed as if the earth was beginning to press in on her from the sides and down on her from above, even upwards from beneath her paws.

'The tunnels go a very long way underground,' said Sandstepper behind her. He obviously expected her to carry on down.

'They may, I don't!' Sheena replied.

She felt like a cork being pushed into a bottle. Soon she would be squeezed, and held fast, and it was too much and she began to panic. She stopped and tried to shuffle backwards.

'Don't do that!' said Sandstepper. 'That's the hard way. If you want to come out, just go a little further in and you'll be able to turn around.'

Sheena forced herself to go forward, although all her instincts were telling her to go back. Sure enough, a little further on and round a slight bend, the tunnel forked again. There was just enough room for her to work her body around so that she was facing back the way she had come. Then she had to back briefly down one of the tunnel branches so that Sandstepper too could turn around. He led her out into the sunshine.

'Thank you,' said Sheena, out of politeness. She hadn't enjoyed that very much.

'Thank *you*,' Sandstepper said, 'for helping Pebble.

'We'll remember you. But we need a name to remember you by. Who are you? *What* are you?'

'I'm Sheena. I'm a domestic cat.'

'A domesticat?'

Sheena didn't quibble. This animal probably had no idea what 'domestic' meant.

'You're Sandstepper, I know that. Are you a mongoose?'

'Yes, a sort of mongoose; but a very special sort.

'I'm a meerkat.'

Chapter Three: Nyegere

First sweet, then bad,
I'm a sudden mood changer;
And it doesn't take much
To turn me into danger.

There was no such thing as a mere cat, as far as Sheena was concerned. She found the name rather insulting.

'No, no, that's not what it means,' Sandstepper assured her. '*Meer* is just an old word for termites; and *kat* is a name mongooses in general are sometimes known by. We eat termites; and we're a kind of mongoose; so we're meerkats. In some places we're called suricates.'

'Er…you eat termites. What else do you eat? Is there any of it round here? And is it juicy?'

Sheena was extremely thirsty by now. She had no hopes of finding water to drink. Something sticky or slimy would have to do instead, as long as it was more than a bit wet.

'Oh, sorry! Are you hungry? I can help you find some food.'

'Runny food, please. I need liquid.

'But I don't mean food that will runny away. I'm too tired to do any chasing.'

'Follow me.'

Sandstepper led Sheena back the way they had come. Sheena was glad about that, since that was the way she now wanted to go...back to where Dad Allen had begun to collect firewood. She was sure she'd be able to find her way to the family campsite from there.

On the short drive from the tents she had tried a new way of travelling by Land Rover. She hadn't taken the risk of attempting to sneak inside the vehicle. Instead she'd climbed up behind one of the rear wheels and draped herself along the back springs on that side. The springs were hard and narrow, and it was a bit like lying on a railway line. She had to hope that the Land Rover wouldn't go over a really big bump. That would have the same effect as a train suddenly arriving. She'd spent a lot of her life trying to make sure she would end up as a fat cat, not a flat cat.

From her uncomfortable position on the cold metal, she had been able to watch the roadside through the wheel arch, as it swept by. She thought she would remember enough of it to be able to get back to the campsite...and Amy...and Thomas.

They descended the slope, and when Sandstepper reached the trees he walked in among them. It was a little darker, a little cooler, in there. He chose a patch of ground between two large tree roots, and began scraping and sniffing. Then he started digging at high speed, and sandy earth flew backwards so that Sheena had to jump to one side to avoid being showered by it. As he dug deeper the earth he was scattering became a darker brown, and smelt damp. Sheena crept forward (from the side) and looked into the hole he was making.

At first there was nothing to be seen through the flurry of Sandstepper's claws, just more sand. Then he paused. Sheena could see some whiteish objects writhing slowly in the bottom of the hole. Sandstepper picked one up, delicately, in his claws, and held it out to her.

'Here. Is this juicy enough for you?'

Nyegere

It was a grub, a fat, glistening, cream-coloured grub, like an albino caterpillar. There were several more twisting and turning in the hole, as if they didn't like the light.

Sheena wasn't sure about the offer. Juicy enough, yes, the grub certainly looked that; but for *her*? No, she wasn't certain this was for her, at all.

'After you,' she said, pretending politeness in order to hide squeamishness.

Snack! The grub was gone. Sandstepper licked his thin lips.

He picked up another and held it out to her.

Sheena had to do it, she had to get some moisture into her body otherwise she'd shrivel. She cautiously took the grub in her mouth. It only wriggled a little bit. She'd have chosen to slurp it down without really tasting it; but it was surprisingly dry on the outside in spite of its glisten. To slurp something that's dry you have to have a certain amount of slurpiness in your mouth to begin with. Sheena didn't have any at all. So she bit.

The grub popped in her mouth, then squelched, then oozed; but it was alright, the taste was alright – slightly sharp, slightly sweet, very refreshing.

In a short space of time they had emptied the hole of grubs. Sheena had quickly got used to the pop, squelch and ooze, got used to the taste (and begun to like it), got used to the trickle down her throat (and welcomed it). She felt much, much better.

'Is this how you always eat, out and about like this?' she asked.

'Yes it is. Our food is usually in small portions – insects and suchlike. It's not easy to carry back to the burrow, so we eat it on the spot. That means our youngsters have to learn to come out and forage for themselves while they're still very small. We don't take much back for them, mainly some specimens to show them what to look for.'

26

'Was Pebble having a foraging lesson?'

'Yes; but he was on the Advanced course – he's older. It's my fault he got hurt. I shouldn't have let him get so far ahead of me among the bushes.'

'What will happen to him?'

'I don't know…I don't know. The Ndugu will do what they can to save him. They're the Sisters – the young females – who know a lot about such things.

'Just being in the burrow and resting in the cool and the quiet will help. Then there are special foods they can give him. There's a particular kind of worm that lives deep in the ground under camelthorn trees – if they can find some in time. But I was surprised that he collapsed so quickly. That wasn't a good sign.'

As they talked they were walking back out through the trees. It looked very bright outside.

'Well if I'm ever this way again…' said Sheena. But she knew she wouldn't be.

'I have to go back now.'

'Pity you couldn't have come further down into Deepden. There's a lot I could have shown you. We lead very interesting lives, we meerkats. We're like a big family.'

'I'm sure there is and I'm sure you do and I'm sure you are. But unless I can find my way back to my own family, *my* life will become *too* interesting,' Sheena said. She'd explained who her family were, and why she needed to be with them. Sandstepper had seemed to understand.

'So I need to start looking now.'

They had reached the edge of the trees. It was time to part. As they stepped out into the sunlight, however, they saw a much larger animal coming towards them.

It was padding purposefully along, following a straight line past the grove of trees and towards the foot of the slope that led up to Deepden. It stopped as soon as it saw them.

It was a very chunky creature, low to the ground. It was also two-tone – its bottom half was black, its top half silver-grey.

Sheena felt something of an affinity with it, since it was near enough black and white, like her. It spoke to Sandstepper in what seemed a friendly enough tone.

'Well then! I'm just on my way to visit you lot. I hear you've had a litter. Thought I'd pay my respects.'

Sandstepper didn't reply, which Sheena found a little strange.

'How's that fine burrow of yours? Have you managed to repair it after the last natural disaster?'

That sounded like a sincere enquiry; but again Sandstepper said nothing. Sheena wondered what the natural disaster had been. It was clear that Sandstepper was not pleased to see this burly animal.

'And who's this?' the newcomer asked (turning to Sheena and smiling with a set of very strong teeth).

'You've hired a security guard, have you? I like the colour but I think you should have gone for the next size up.'

The animal laughed as he spoke. It was a deep laugh, but was it a friendly one? Sheena didn't think so. She hadn't found it a very friendly comment. She was beginning to be rather put off, also, by the creature's small, piggy eyes and long, piggy snout…and also by its large, doggy teeth, which it showed much too often.

'So tell me about the new arrivals. How many?'

'I don't think you need to know that, Nyegere,' said Sandstepper coldly.

So there *was* something wrong.

'You're right, my friend, I don't. I'm sure there'll be enough of them to make my journey worthwhile, thank you. Even if there's only one, the babysitter will stay at home to protect it when I come knocking on the door and the rest of you run away.'

The animal now grinned, but horribly.

'So I'm guaranteed two good chews at least.'

Niceness was turning suddenly to nastiness. It seemed, however, that this Nyegere wanted something from Sandstepper.

'I'd have thought you yourself would be more pleased to see me, you know. The more of your tribe I kill, the better chance failures like you will have of becoming somebody. You'll be able to climb further up the pile because I'll have knocked off some of those above you. Who knows, maybe one day you'll get breeding rights and be able to father your own litter.

'So how about this. You don't run back to the burrow and tell them I'm coming. Just stay here in the shade instead. Then your almighty Leader and his Chosen One won't have a chance to escape and I'll do you a favour; and my journey will have been *really* worthwhile.'

Sheena didn't understand all of that. She didn't need to. This animal intended to attack the burrow, one way or the other. Pebble for one would be in no fit state to run away, whether or not the meerkats were warned.

She couldn't believe, though, that Sandstepper would fall in with the animal's plans. His meerkat tribe seemed to matter far too much to him.

She was right.

'No. I don't do deals with honey badgers. So how about this instead?'

Honey badgers! Sheena had heard about honey badgers, and their unpredictable moods and their great strength...and their very large appetites.

Sandstepper obviously knew this particular honey badger well. He now sprang in front of the much bigger animal and began to perform a solo version of the group dance that had taken place on top of the Deepden mound. It was almost as impressive, with much scratching, jumping and pounding, much growling and snarling and spitting. A dense cloud of dust rose up and partly hid the meerkat. Once again there was the illusion of a violent forwards charge, but no actual forwards movement.

Except from Nyegere. He suddenly performed a real forwards charge and side-swiped Sandstepper with a heavy paw. The blow knocked Sandstepper off his feet. He got up onto all fours straight away and tried to run for the trees; but he was obviously injured, and was holding a front paw off the ground. He would normally have been able to outrun the bulkier animal (which was probably why the latter had tried to talk him into a special arrangement), but not now. Nyegere set off after him.

It was up to Sheena to do something.

She ran too; but she didn't run for the trees, she ran for the slope; and she didn't run as quickly as she could have done.

She had decided that her only hope of saving Sandstepper was to draw Nyegere away.

'Don't worry, Sandstepper!' she called. 'I'll warn them! They'll have plenty of time to put The Plan into operation!'

There was no reply from Sandstepper. There was no such thing as The Plan either, of course; there was only *her* Plan.

Her Plan was to make the honey badger choose – between an injured meerkat in the bush and several meerkats in the burrow.

Nyegere paused. He was obviously thinking, as Sheena had intended he should.

If he pursued Sandstepper into the trees, this strange little black-and-white animal now escaping would reach the burrow well ahead of him; and the thought that the meerkats had a Plan worried him a little. He knew how tricky those creatures could be.

If on the other hand he ignored the meerkat he had crippled, and went straight to the burrow – well, this runaway cat-thing didn't seem able to run away very quickly, and even if he couldn't catch it and clobber it he would reach Deepden hot on its heels.

So that was the better option; and that was the one he chose.

He called out in a voice much more powerful than the one he had used to negotiate.

'Alright, Suricate: I'll find you another time and side-swipe you the other way. Then we'll have some fun.

'Alright, Securicat!' he shouted after Sheena. 'Let's see how fast you can go!'

He turned away from Sandstepper and began to run heavily after the little black-and-white animal escaping towards the slope.

Chapter Four: Ncha

You'll find me in the end
(Of the final joint),
But you'll wish you hadn't –
If you get my point.

Sheena had saved Sandstepper for the moment, but that was about all. Even that achievement wasn't wholly secure. If she ran too fast and Nyegere realised too soon that he could not keep up with her, that she would reach Deepden a long way ahead of him and give the meerkats lots of warning, he might decide to cut his losses, double back, hunt for the crippled Sandstepper and make a meal of him.

If she ran too slowly, however…

She didn't know how fast her pursuer could move. He had great, strong legs, but his body looked cumbersome. How easily would he get up the slope?

She tested him. When she got to the bottom of the slope she deliberately slowed down, as if she was having difficulty in the deeper sand. Nyegere gained on her. Then when he too reached the gradient Sheena increased her speed a little, just in case his strength carried him easily upwards. Nyegere increased his, and the gap between them narrowed. Sheena ran a little faster, Nyegere ran a little faster; but Sheena could now hear him panting. She risked a look back.

He was a ferocious sight, with his intent, piggy eyes and frightening teeth, and he was still running strongly; but his teeth were now partly hidden by his tongue, which hung out over them, and he was beginning to gasp.

Sheena was afraid he was about to give up, turn around and head back down towards the trees; so she allowed her paws to scutter in the sand, which brought her almost to a halt.

Suddenly Nyegere was within what might be his leaping range (although he didn't look like a leaper). When Sheena tried to speed up again, her paws slipped and kept slipping, and for an awful moment she thought she had misjudged things. She was doing what the meerkats had done on their mound, going through the motions of running but standing still. She dug her paws in more deeply and got going once more, although heavily. At the same time she heard the clash of teeth just behind her. If she'd had a full-length tail she'd have been caught.

Nyegere's near-success was enough to carry him to the top of the slope; but Sheena took care that he didn't get as close a second time. She did continue to control her speed, though, so that it seemed as if he *might* get as close if he tried a *little* harder…

Once they were on level ground she ran steadily, still careful not to get too far ahead of him until they were so far from the trees, and near enough to Deepden, that he would be very unlikely to turn around and go back. Then she increased her speed, and the gap between them widened. By the time she came within sight of the central mound he was a long way behind. She had bought some time. How could she use it?

The solitary meerkat on sentry duty barked as soon as he saw her; then he barked frantically when he saw who was in the distance behind her. The other meerkats came tumbling out of the mound and jumped up on top, ready to do their war-dance.

As Sheena came close they all started shouting at once, at her and to each other.

'Where's Sandstepper?'

'Look! Oh Look!'

'Don't look!'

'Why have you brought that great beast here?'

'Is Sandstepper dead?'

'Let's run!'

'We're lost! There isn't time to evacuate!'

'You've betrayed us! We thought you were our friend!'

'He'll destroy the burrow like he did last time!'

'Please help us!'

'Let's do The Jump!'

'There's no point! Nyegere always sees through our tricks!'

'He'll eat the pups!'

'And some of us!'

'Not me!'

The last meerkat to speak, a smaller individual with very dark fur, jumped down and ran off slowly in a scatter of sand, away from the mound, away from Sheena, away from the approaching honey badger.

The other meerkats moved to the edge of the mound. They obviously didn't know whether to follow their instincts and run away as well or follow their instincts and dive into the tunnels and hide.

'Wait! Before you follow any of your instincts, listen to me.'

As she increased her distance from the pursuing Nyegere, Sheena had thought up an extension to her Plan. That, to begin with, had been only to save Sandstepper. Now it was to save Pebble, and whatever baby meerkats were deep in the burrow, and whatever other meerkats stayed around to be saved.

She explained her idea quickly; and the meerkats seemed to understand it. Only one of them needed to help her, but two of them chose to. One was Tuft. She suspected that was partly so that he could keep an eye on her.

The other meerkats very readily disappeared into the side-entrances of the mound.

Sheena led the way into the main entrance: she, who had become so quickly afraid in the tunnels earlier, led the way. The two meerkats turned, as they had been instructed, into the chamber on the right, and disappeared from sight. There wasn't time to stop and check that they knew exactly what more they were supposed to do.

Sheena forced herself to go on to where the tunnel narrowed, and further. When she had almost reached the fork she turned around so that she was facing back towards the tunnel entrance. She thought she heard the movement of other meerkats behind her. They must have raced back in this direction through the tunnels from the side entrances. So there *were* some brave animals among them, some who were prepared to stand and fight if Nyegere got past her.

Sheena was determined he would not, not until something else had happened. She was going to be a cork after all, a little black-and-white stopper blocking the tunnel against a big black-and-white bully.

She knew she would be able to do that only temporarily. Nyegere was designed for digging, with a flat head, powerful front legs and large hooked claws. The earth was soft. He would be able to dig around her in no time; or he would simply dig through her, ripping her flesh in passing.

She could hear him now, hear the thud of his paws as he arrived at the main entrance: he was not an animal to use side doors; and he didn't knock after all. The tunnel darkened as he thrust his large head and shoulders into the opening. He began to dig immediately. Sheena couldn't see him, but she could hear his grunts and the shushing of the sand as he pulled it back past his body.

The tunnel continued to get darker as he worked his way in towards her. She could smell him now, smell his hot fur and his nasty breath.

After turning around she had stayed in that slightly wider part of the tunnel. She needed to be able to use her sharp little claws if she had to. She would try her sharp little words first, however.

When the flat end of Nyegere's pale, wet snout showed around the bend in the tunnel, Sheena called out to him.

'So you made it after all! I thought we'd have to come and carry you over the last part. You're really out of condition, you know! Time you went on a healthier diet – roots and shoots and things.

'Soon you're going to get tired and then you'll get stuck. Then *we'll* have some fun with *you!*'

She had remembered his last cruel words to Sandstepper, and wondered how the injured meerkat was faring.

Her words had the wrong effect on Nyegere. The shushing of sand and the grunting both increased, and suddenly his whole head appeared. His eyes burned in the half-darkness.

'You're talking nonsense, little Securicat,' he snarled.

(She feared she was.)

'Is that how you hope to earn your keep? Do you think you can slow me down with silly threats?

'And did you think you'd tire me out by making me run here? I may not be the fastest thing on four legs, but I can keep going all day, and all night if need be. You've seen me run; now watch

37

me dig!'

His large front claws appeared on either side of his head, and began to haul sand away from around it in great backwards scoops. Soon his broad shoulders were visible, and soon after that he was able to lever himself towards her, helped no doubt by his strong back legs pushing his whole body forward.

He was well past the side chamber by now. The two meerkats should be able to do what they had to; but there was no indication that anything was happening behind the honey badger.

'Wait!' said Sheena. Nyegere was coming closer with every scoop of sand and every heave of his body. Sheena was very afraid. She could retreat either tail-first or head-first down one of the two tunnels behind her, but she knew she was very likely to get jammed tight quite quickly. Once that happened, she would not be able to defend herself and would be at Nyegere's mercy (and she was sure he didn't have any). At least here, where she was, she had sufficient room to move her front legs. She focused her attention on his glistening snout. That's where she would have to strike with her claws if she wanted to stop him.

'Wait why?' Nyegere snarled.

Then he found out.

His head suddenly hit the roof above him and his dark little eyes opened wide. So did his mouth with its shining teeth, and a great roar came out, together with a blast of hot, angry breath, so powerful that Sheena felt she was being forced further down the tunnel.

'Arr...rrr...rrr!'

It was a terrifying noise. Sheena's ears rang, and she was temporarily deafened. She expected him to lunge for her in pain and rage. Instead he jerked backwards. He roared again, even louder and even longer.

'Arrr...rrr...rrr...rrr!'

Whatever had hurt him the first time had hurt him a second time, even more. Sheena steeled herself for an attack. If he came forward now she knew she wouldn't be able to stop him. The damage she could do from in front, to his tender nose, would be nothing compared with the pain that had just been inflicted from behind. Her claws were not full of poison like a scorpion's sting.

Nyegere had a much larger body mass than Pebble, so Sheena didn't expect to see any symptoms beyond Number One. It seemed however that intense pain at the sting site, beginning immediately, might be enough. The badger's great head was sharply withdrawn as he pulled himself backwards in an explosion of sand. His roaring continued, but became muffled as he humped himself back towards the entrance with great thuds of his body on the tunnel's sandy floor.

Then there was an even louder thud, and Nyegere's roaring was silenced, as the roof of the tunnel fell on Sheena.

Chapter Five: Usingizi

I fill the gap
Between day and day.
When I enfold you
You feel you've gone away.

By the time the meerkats dug her out, Sheena had nearly died, and Nyegere was long gone. While she was recovering, Tuft took great delight in telling her how the other symptoms of scorpion envenomation had appeared in the honey badger, one by one. Some of the meerkats had followed Nyegere for a short distance, jeering, as he stumbled away.

The funniest part had been when he had tried to threaten them, over his twitching shoulder. Dysarthria had turned, 'I'll chomp you and chew you and spit you in the sand!' into a pathetic, 'Ileshomyou…anshewyou…anshpiyou…inthshan!'

Then he had an attack of Symptom Number 10.

'I don't think I'll ever be afraid of him again!' said Tuft.

He noticed that Sheena was having difficulty breathing. Her ribs had been crushed by the heavy fall of sand, and she had been trapped for what seemed a very long time until she felt claws digging away a space around her head. By then she had breathed in quite a lot of what she had been buried under.

'We need to help you away from here. We can't go back. The main entrance has collapsed. We'll have to go down.'

41

Didn't down mean narrower? Sheena had had enough of narrow.

'Don't worry. Just past the fork the main tunnel widens out. We keep the passages in the upper parts of the burrow as narrow as possible to stop animals any bigger than us from sneaking in. Only diggers like Nyegere are a threat to us in here, and sometimes slitherers – but we can usually take care of *them*.'

Sheena hesitated, but there was no choice in the matter. She allowed herself to be led (with an occasional helping push from behind when she began to stick) down the tunnel. She could move only slowly because of her ribs and her breathing. She coughed every now and again and brought up sand into her mouth.

The tunnel did gradually become wider, but it also went downwards more steeply. She felt uneasy heading so far underground, with that increasing weight of sand above her. What if the whole tunnel system collapsed?

Other tunnels branched off, left and right, and some of them presumably led back up to the surface, but most were too narrow for her. Sometimes, too, there were what seemed to be more chambers off to one side or the other.

She continued to follow Tuft down into the deeper darkness – where she could still see, of course, once her cat's eyes had adjusted. There were meerkats behind her, but she could not tell how many.

They kept going for a long time, with Sheena growing more and more anxious the further down they went. Then the tunnel floor levelled off and she found herself in a much more open space (open, that is, except for upwards: the roof was too low for her liking). Other tunnels led off in several directions. She stayed close to Tuft. If she had been left alone now she would have had no idea which tunnel to take. One of Dad Allen's favourite philosophical sayings was, 'The best way out is always through.' As far as Sheena was concerned, the best way out was always up, when you were deep underground. But which was an Up tunnel?

'Hello there! Hello!'

The voice came from behind her, but not from one of the meerkats who had followed from above. When she turned round she saw that to the right of the tunnel she had just come down there was quite a large open chamber. A meerkat was curled up on its floor, with his head raised, looking at her. She recognised Pebble.

She began to reply, was going to say all the right things, such as, 'I'm very pleased to see you're over your dysarthria,' and, 'How's your paraesthesia?' All that came out, however, was a wheeze. Then she started to cough, violently. Her throat filled with sand and she felt she was about to choke once more. Soon she had coughed out most of the air in her lungs, but she couldn't breathe in for fear of sucking the sand back down. She was in deep distress. Her head began to spin.

'Thump!'

One of the several meerkats who had come down the tunnel behind her now leapt onto her back and started to do a therapeutic version of the war dance.

'Thumpetty-thump!' his little feet went, on either side of her spine.

'Thumpetty-thump!' his little head went also, on the roof just above him, bringing down more sand.

'Coughetty-cough!' went Sheena with the last of her air, and a plug of sand burst out of her windpipe and scattered over the ground in front of her. She took a sand-free breath.

The meerkat jumped down from her back, his head perhaps

even flatter now.

'Thank you! Thank you!' Sheena said.

She was still wheezy, but she was still alive. She might not have been. Having something stuck in a passageway inside you, she decided, could be much worse than being stuck in a passageway on the outside.

'You need to rest,' said Tuft.

Sheena did feel rather unwell. Her lungs were heavy, she still could not take a full breath, and her throat was raw and rasping.

'The Ndugu will be able to give you something to help you breathe more easily. Why don't you lie down here?'

He led the way into the chamber where Pebble was.

Now that Sheena could look more closely at the young meerkat she realised that he, too, had just survived a truly nasty event. It seemed nearly all the life had been drawn out of him, as if the scorpion, having injected him with venom, had sucked out his spirit as it withdrew its sting. His fur looked dry and lifeless, and his eyes were dull.

In spite of his weakness he was very interested in what had happened up above. Sheena (stopping every now and again when she became breathless) told him what the Plan had been. She had to rely on Tuft, however, to tell him what had actually happened.

The two meerkats had taken longer than expected to chew off the tough tail from the scorpion specimen in the side-chamber and manoeuvre it into position behind Nyegere. Then when they had tried to jab the sting into him they had discovered that his thick fur protected him too well: they had managed to get it no more than a little way through his skin – enough to hurt him but not enough to hurt him badly. So they pulled it out in order to try again. Luckily, he had then lunged backwards in pain after the first prod and driven the sting hard into his own rump, forcing the rest of its venom deep into his flesh. That's when he had *really* gone backwards, trampling the meerkats into the sand in his haste to get out of there, and turning round so violently while he was still in the burrow that he brought the whole roof down on top of them all.

Just as Tuft was finishing his story two new meerkats appeared from one of the tunnels. They were carrying leaves in their mouths.

'Here are two of the Ndugu!' said Tuft.

'They've brought something for you.'

The two female meerkats were called Curl and Fara. Fara was well beyond being a pup, but obviously small for her age.

Later, when Sheena and Pebble fell to talking about names (she was interested in his) she would learn that meerkats identified each other in several ways. One of the most important was by smell, since their close-up eyesight wasn't very good, as already noted. Sheena decided that meerkats on guard duty should be called scentinels.

Another was by the sound of their voices.

'You'll soon meet a meerkat called Twizzle,' said Pebble. 'She's called that because she twizzles on and on, all the time.'

Sometimes a meerkat had a distinguishing feature (like Tuft's hair) or skill (like Sandstepper's ability to tread where others sank). That was what they became known for, and that was what gave them their names.

'If you were a meerkat you'd probably be called Stump,' said Tuft.

Sheena wasn't terribly sensitive about her tail, most of which she had lost in an accident when she was quite young; but she didn't much like the sound of *Stump*.

Curl's name was easy to understand, then. Meerkat tails were long, with black tips, and usually hung in a loop down towards the ground then up again. When the animals became excited or anxious or angry their tails sprang up to the perpendicular like little flagpoles, with their feelings of the moment flapping away at the top. Curl's tail was always in a graceful curve behind her: she never seemed to get excited or anxious, and certainly not angry.

Fara's name, though – that was a bit more problematical. Pebble had to explain.

'Fara never finishes anything. When she was young and food was being brought back to the burrow for her, she would take a few bites and leave the rest. Even when she began to go out and seek food for herself, it was the same – she'd dig up a worm, eat most of it and leave the last bite. Some lazy youngsters took to following her round, since they knew they could make a good meal from her leftovers.

'So her mother decided she didn't deserve a whole name and gave her only part of one. She said that when Fara learnt to end what she'd begun, then she could have the whole of her name.

'She hasn't learnt to do that yet. Didn't you notice?'

Sheena had been aware of Fara's strange way of speaking. She left her sentences uncompleted.

'We've brought you these leaves so that you can...' she'd said to Sheena, laying the leaves at her feet. Then it was as if she'd forgotten what she was going to say, or had begun to think about something else entirely.

Curl had had to finish the explanation for her.

'...so that you can chew them. They will give off a vapour you can breathe in. That will help repair the damage the grains of sand have done to your throat and lungs.'

'When I come next time I'll...,' Fara said to Pebble, and he was left to work out for himself what she had intended to say.

46

Then she began to groom Pebble's leg. She parted his short fur carefully with her claws and nibbled at his skin.

Sheena knew about grooming. She had been groomed herself by a friendly little baboon (in the midst of some very unfriendly ones) the first time she had come to Baragandiri.

Fara was finding the small parasites digging into Pebble's flesh (most meerkats had some) and nipping them off with her sharp teeth. It was a way of soothing him and making him feel more secure – part of the healing process.

Then she suddenly stopped and wandered out of the chamber, leaving Pebble with his leg sticking up ridiculously in the air.

Fara's full name was Faraway, since that is where she seemed to go when she drifted off in the middle of saying or doing something.

'That's not really fair,' said Sheena. 'Once she's learnt to concentrate on things until she's finished doing them, she won't go faraway any more and she won't deserve the name.'

'Then she'll be able to have a new name, one of her own choosing,' said Pebble.

'So what about *your* name?' asked Sheena. That after all was where the conversation had started. She had decided that there were worse things to do than rest here a little longer, now that she had become somewhat used to being underground, so she had settled down next to Pebble and begun to talk with him.

She had chewed the leaves as directed by Curl. They had a slightly bitter taste, and gave off a sharp, herby aroma. When she breathed in through her mouth she felt the air strangely cool on the back of her throat, then strangely warming when it got to her lungs. It soon became easier to breathe, and the air no longer rasped against her throat on its way in.

Her ribs still hurt, though.

'Oh…when I was growing up I found it very difficult to make other meerkats understand what I was saying. My lips and tongue and teeth didn't work very well together. So the Ndugu (the females who were Ndugu then, I mean) made me keep a pebble in my mouth. My lips and tongue and teeth had to cooperate very hard to produce any sounds at all. Next I had to force them to make sense. After a few weeks the Ndugu let me take the pebble out; and I found I could speak normally. I buried the pebble, but I decided to keep the name.

'When I was stung by the scorpion and couldn't talk properly, I was afraid that my problem had come back. That was almost worse than the pain. But I still know where the pebble is…'

Just as he was coming to the end of his story (which he'd told very clearly), sounds of a disturbance drifted down one of the tunnels. Sheena and Pebble had been left alone, and she was suddenly fearful that something bad was going to happen. They were in no fit state to defend themselves, and they would not be able to run away. (The thought of rushing off into that dark labyrinth terrified her anyway.)

From where they lay they could see the mouth of the tunnel down which the sounds were coming. The noise drew closer and became more worrisome; but then Sheena was able to make out meerkat talk; and Pebble, who had tried to sit up, lay back down again.

'It's alright,' he said.

A large meerkat, walking with difficulty, entered the central chamber, where all the tunnels met. It was Sandstepper.

Fara was behind him, and spoke to him as he got close to them.

'Just lie down next to Pebble and rest until…' she said.

Then she left.

48

All three of them rested, and rested some more, in what had become something like an underground hospital ward.

They had plenty of opportunity to talk. Sandstepper told them how he had hidden among the trees until he was sure Nyegere had followed Sheena. Then he had begun to climb slowly and painfully up the slope, stopping every now and again. He knew what Nyegere intended, and he could do nothing to stop him. So he was rather puzzled a short while later when, in the distance, he saw Nyegere coming back down towards the trees, walking strangely, with a little hop and a scuttle every now and again as if he was trying to get away from something invisible behind him that kept jabbing him. Sandstepper hid in some shrubs while Nyegere went by.

'He was whimpering,' Sandstepper said.

'Now I know why.'

Sandstepper was fine apart from his leg, which was badly bruised but not broken. Pebble was fine apart from his general weakness and a swollen cheek. Sheena was fine as long as she took only shallow breaths.

Sandstepper apologised to Pebble for not looking after him more carefully.

Pebble apologised to Sandstepper for rushing on ahead and getting himself stung.

'That's me all over!' he said. I'm just too eager!'

Then he spoke to Sheena.

'It all has to do with that slow start I had because of my mouth not working properly. I've always felt I had to catch up; so I often run on ahead, and try to do things my own way.'

'Yes, you're very aheadstrong. That's why I was asked to take care of you. I should have stayed closer to you,' said Sandstepper.

Sandstepper and Pebble then both apologised to Sheena for

the danger she had been placed in.

'Enough of this saying sorry!' said Curl, bustling in. 'If you feel you have to say sorry to everybody you'll start to feel sorry for yourselves because you have to say sorry to everybody. Soon you'll be saying sorry for saying sorry.'

Fara had come in behind her.

'It's time for…' she said, slowly.

It soon became evident what it was time for. It was time for the meerkats to sleep.

Sounds rolled down several of the tunnels and spilled out into the open area in a confused jumble so that it was impossible to tell which sound had come from where. Then meerkats started to arrive, first from this tunnel, then from that. They tumbled out into the central chamber like the sounds had done and flopped down on the ground together so that they quickly became a pile. There were more than ten of them but less than twenty: it was hard to tell once they were mixed up. Sheena didn't see Tuft anywhere.

It seemed that they were deliberately lying on top of one another to form a meerkat pyramid. Sheena wondered if this was the beginning of some sort of game, and the meerkats at the bottom of the pile would try to wriggle out from underneath without causing the pyramid to collapse, then climb up on top before being climbed on in their turn and gradually sinking to the bottom again. A game like that could go on all night.

For it *was* night, Sheena realised. Curl and Fara settled down on either side of Pebble and Sandstepper (who were already lying close together).

'Would you like …?' said Fara to Sheena; then she shut her eyes and went to sleep.

'Would you like to come close to us?' said Curl, who was still awake.

'It gets very cold down here at night. We always sleep close together.'

There was no sign of the meerkats at the base of the pyramid trying to wriggle free. On the contrary, they all had their eyes shut and were lying very still. They looked as if they had partially melted together. Sheena thought she could hear something between a large sigh and a large snore – a single sound that came from the whole pile, breathing with one breath.

'This isn't the whole tribe,' said Curl.

'There are other sleeping-places, and other sleeping-piles.'

The four meerkats in the chamber with her were not in a pile, but they were snuggled up very close.

'Join us!' said Pebble, sleepily.

Sheena moved over and lay down alongside Curl. That meant

she was in touch with Pebble (through Curl). She felt quite close to him in other ways as well.

She was also in touch with Sandstepper (through Pebble and Curl) and even Fara (through all of the other three). She could feel warmth radiating from their bodies. They too seemed to be breathing in and out together. As she fell asleep she could feel her own breathing (slightly wheezy, still) falling into the same rhythm.

Chapter Six: Maadui

Not nice,
Not friend,
You or them
In the end.

It was very bright. The sharp sun was shining directly into Sheena's eyes – shining upwards into them, since she was standing on top of the mound, and the sun had just come up over the flat horizon.

There were meerkats on either side of her – meerkats from among those who had slept near her in the pile. On smaller mounds nearby stood other meerkats, who must have slept somewhere else.

They all *had* slept, she knew, because they all looked sleepy still.

She had woken just as the last of the pile had disentangled themselves and set off up the main tunnel. Curl and Fara had arrived at the same time, with some small insects, crunchy on the outside but good and watery inside. Sheena had found them most refreshing. There must have been a supply nearby, for the two Ndugu quickly went and came back with more for Pebble and Sandstepper.

There was a strong, sharp smell of urine in the large chamber where the meerkats had been, as if they'd slept so soundly through the night that absolutely nothing could wake them. 'I must remember never to sleep at the bottom of a pile of meerkats,' Sheena thought.

The two Ndugu persuaded her to leave the chamber and go to the surface with them, once they had checked that she felt well enough to do so.

'We need to go up for Sunwake,' Curl said.

'Then we'll come back down and warm Pebble and Sandstepper.'

Pebble and Sandstepper, it seemed, needed more rest, and Sheena had heard Curl and Fara talking about finding some special food for them.

'We'll have to go to Edgemound and then past the...,' said Fara.

Sheena had followed Curl's swaying tail up a surprisingly short but steep tunnel that brought them out on the side of a small heap of sand a little way in front of the main mound, on top of which the meerkats from the chamber were already standing.

From this distance the meerkats looked exactly alike, and they were in identical postures – sharp faces pointed at the sun, front legs tucked into their sides, front paws dangling down over their chests. They resembled a row of tennis spectators, waiting for the game to begin. The illusion was reinforced by the black circles around their eyes, which looked like sunglasses. (Sheena learned later that the black circles did indeed absorb some of the sun's glare, and made it easier for the meerkats to see in harsh light.) All it would take would be for the bright white sun to begin bouncing back and forward along the horizon, and the meerkat heads would swivel, and swivel back, and swivel again, precisely in time with its movement. Would the meerkats clap with their long paws when a point was scored?

Curl led her towards the mound. As they drew close a younger meerkat at one end of the group slowly closed his eyes, lurched, and fell off the mound. He landed with a thump on the ground and lay there for a moment with his eyes still closed; then he struggled awake and upright, and climbed back up to where the other meerkats were. None of them had paid any attention to him, as if this was quite a usual occurrence.

Several of them did, however, move aside and make room for Curl, Fara and Sheena when they too climbed up on top.

'Welcome to Sunwake,' said Curl. 'You will soon be warm. Your black fur will warm up very quickly.'

Sheena hadn't felt especially cold, but then her coat was much thicker than the meerkats', as well as much darker (where it wasn't white). The skin on the meerkats' flat chests, however, was grey for the most part, and almost bare of fur. Their chests therefore acted like solar panels, absorbing the sun's rays and helping warm the rest of their bodies. So they stuck them out, and stood there blinking, suffering the light for the sake of the heat, until they were fully warm and fully awake.

The sun turned gradually from white to yellow, and its rays grew stronger. Soon the meerkats' day could begin.

There was more to Sunwake than that, however. The meerkats were absorbing things other than warmth from the sun, and there was a larger renewal going on. Their spirits were being raised along with their temperatures.

They did not move for quite a long while. Their stillness as they stood there, their intense concentration, made it seem as if they were expecting a message.

They must have received one, somehow, because they suddenly became invigorated. As if a signal had been given, they jumped down from the mound and began to mix with one another in a most family fashion. The same thing happened at the other mounds.

Dad Allen sometimes (not often) talked about feeling chirpy in the morning. The meerkats, as they got ready to go about their daily business, were altogether chir*ruppy*. They greeted each other with warbly tweets and whistles, not unlike early morning birds. Much licking of each others' fur went on, and some grooming. Two meerkats simply stood clasping each other. Sheena saw the tall Tuft being rubbed up against by a slightly shorter, plumper female meerkat. To one side there was a group of youngsters, who had not been able to climb up onto the mound but had nevertheless warmed up enough to be able to romp around: they were jumping on each other, wrestling, and pretending to nip each other with their sharp little teeth.

It all seemed very much a celebration of the new day. Sheena herself, standing alongside the meerkats on the mound, had felt the sun's warmth on her fur; and as it sank in it seemed to call forth an answering warmth from inside her body, a conviction that all was right in the world. She would be back with the Allens soon, she was sure.

Curl had joined in the meerkat activity, Fara too up to a point: Sheena noticed her reach out towards a very young meerkat walking on all fours towards her. It looked for a moment as if she was going to stroke it on the head, but her paw didn't quite get there. The young meerkat continued walking past her, and she was left with her paw hanging in the air as if she'd forgotten what she was going to do with it.

'Do you always start the day like this?' Sheena asked Curl.

'Yes, of course,' said Curl.

'Some of us may not live to see the end of it, so we make sure we enjoy its beginning. Sunwake helps us to do that.'

Tuft came over to Sheena, followed by the female meerkat who had been rubbing up against him. As they arrived Curl stepped back, and Sheena sensed respect in her manner.

'Thank you, little cat,' Tuft said.

'And I'm sorry. I was suspicious of you at first. I should not have been.'

'Yes you should,' said the female meerkat, who Sheena learned later was called Moon. Sheena didn't feel that the comment was particularly directed against her.

'It's your job to be suspicious, Tuft. These are dangerous times for the Duwara. Who knows what the Utongo will do next? It would suit them very well to have a dunzi in Deepden.'

Sheena didn't know what the Duwara and the Utongo were, but she knew what a dunzi was. She'd been one, once. It was a spy.

'No, we don't think *you're* a Utongo dunzi,' said Moon, turning to her. 'You've done too many good things for us.'

Tuft and this other meerkat seemed to have leadership roles in what turned out to be the Duwara tribe of meerkats. They were the number one male and the number one female, the only meerkats allowed to mate and have pups – officially, that is.

'Utongo? What are the Utongo?' Sheena asked. Since she had almost been accused of being one of them she wanted to know what they were.

It was Tuft who answered her.

'The Utongo are another meerkat tribe. They are our enemies.

'Once they were only our neighbours. We fought now and again, but only in a small way. Neighbours do that. Now, however, we are at war with them.'

'Why?'

'Because they want to take over Deepden. They want to take over *us*, and make us like them.'

'But you *are* like them: you're all meerkats!'

Sheena felt she was stating the obvious; but then what did she know? She had not seen these Utongo. Perhaps they were purple and walked backwards.

Tuft paused, then spoke slowly and with great weight.

'The Utongo are not like us. They live under a different sun.'

Chapter Seven: Nungunungu

If I told you what's on my back
You might say I was a bird;
But if you saw me flying
You'd think I looked absurd.

If you attacked me from the front
You could just have a chance,
But if you leapt on me from behind
You'd do a merry dance.

They live under a different sun. Sheena tried to decide what Tuft could have meant by that, as she began to work her way back down through the tunnel system to say goodbye to Pebble and Sandstepper. She had not been able to ask Tuft, since after his strange statement he and his mate had turned away to go down to the nursery chamber where their new-born pups were.

They would be off foraging soon, with the rest of the tribe, and wanted to check on the litter before they left them in the care of a pup-sitter. Moon had explained that meerkats lose a lot of their body weight overnight, and need to make it up again quickly the following day…so their daily routine consists largely of lots of snacks, and they set off hunting (rather a grand term for it, since it mainly involves digging) as soon as they've completed their Sunwake ritual.

As Moon was talking, Sheena had watched Curl and Fara leave the mound and cross over to the smaller pile of sand the three of them had emerged from earlier. They must be going to take some of the sun's warmth, held in their hot fur, down to Pebble and Sandstepper. By the time Tuft and Moon had left, Curl and Fara had disappeared into the tunnel system.

Sheena was fairly confident that she would be able to find her own way to the central chamber. That was just as well, for when she looked around she could see lots of meerkats but they were already some distance away, in a wide circle among the mounds and moving further off all the time, scratching, sniffing, digging and grubbing as they went.

The tunnels did not seem so forbidding, now. The upper levels would still be a tight squeeze for her, but she knew things would get easier further down. So she trotted over to the tunnel Curl and Fara had used, and set off on what should have been quite a short journey.

She never knew where she had gone wrong, but it must have been at one of the junctions. Things always look different when you see them from the opposite side, and that's particularly true of places where roads meet.

She had travelled quite some way, sure she was going in the right direction – or rather directions, since the tunnels kept turning to left and to right. She had had to choose between one tunnel and another on a couple of occasions, but each time had been certain she knew which was the correct one.

Then she found she was walking in a straight line for much further than she remembered doing on the way up. She came to a large rock, where the tunnel went off at a sharp angle. She did not remember that. Just past the rock there was a short drop over another, smaller rock in the tunnel floor. If they had come that

60

way earlier, they would have had to leap up to the higher level.

So she knew she was lost. There was no point in turning round and going back: she could remember no distinguishing marks in the tunnels behind her that might tell her where she was.

She did not panic. All tunnels led to the outside sooner or later, she trusted. 'What goes down must come up!' she told herself. Provided she did not choose one that became altogether too narrow for her, all she had to do was keep going in the same direction, and she would begin to see daylight – dim at first, then strengthening as she got nearer the exit. Then she could seek help in finding her way to where she wanted to be; or she could just leave Deepden altogether without saying goodbye, and head for the Allen campsite – where she *really* wanted to be.

The tunnels themselves were deserted, since all the meerkats except the one looking after the pups had gone off for breakfast, then breakfast, followed by breakfast.

As soon as she realised how thoroughly lost she was, however, the tunnels became frightening again, even though she thought they were empty. She began to hear noises from openings she passed – a whisper from this one, a patter of paws from that, the thud of sand falling from another. She began to hurry, now wanting to get back to the surface as quickly as possible. When she tried to run, however, her back scraped along the roof and brought down clumps of sand, which frightened her even more.

For every left turn she took from then on, she took a right one when the opportunity arose. If a tunnel seemed to curve to the right, she chose the next fork to the left. She would soon be outside, she hoped, and she would be very interested to see where she was in relation to the main mound. How far had she come?

Tunnel kept on leading into tunnel, however, and she became more and more anxious. Might it have been better after all to turn round and try to retrace her steps? It was too late for that now. The only good thing was that she did not seem to be going any deeper. In fact, for the last little while she felt to have been walking upwards.

For a time it was quiet again. The only noise to be heard was the patter of her own paws on the compacted sand, and a bit of wheeze in her breathing. Then, after another long, straight stretch of tunnel with no branches off, she began to hear a new sound, coming from up ahead.

It was a dry rattling. She stopped immediately. The rattling stopped. She started to move forward again. The rattling started again.

Didn't some snakes rattle? Having tangled with hissing and spitting and squeezing snakes she wanted nothing more to do with snakes of any kind.

There was a bend ahead. The sound was coming from just around it. Sheena stepped forward cautiously, one paw at a time. The tunnel was suddenly narrower here – a rock stuck out into it – and she had to do a bit of squeezing and give a final wriggle to get past the obstruction. Then she was able to move towards the bend, slowly, slowly.

She was concentrating so hard on the curve of the wall as she approached it that she paid no attention to what was underfoot until she felt a shifting and crunching under her paws. She was walking on a carpet of loose objects that rolled, clacked and clattered as she disturbed them.

They were bones, lots of bones, enough to make several whole animals if you were to put them all back together. For they had *been* together, once, had *been* whole animals. What ferocious creature had dismantled them like this, and by means of what terrible teeth and claws and jaws?

Perhaps she should go back after all, if only as far as the last junction (she would need to go back backwards, since the tunnel at this point was too narrow for her to turn around).

Then the rattling started again, much louder and closer. She could see what was round the corner now; but that was odd – she hadn't moved at all from a moment ago when she could see nothing of what was round the corner.

Then she realised that what was round the corner was coming towards her.

It looked like a very large, straggly broom, with all of its long bristles – mainly black with a few white ones among them – pointing forwards. It filled the whole tunnel, and was being pushed steadily in her direction.

'Is it spring cleaning time?' she wondered.

'It does need a good sweep in here.'

Suddenly, with a rattle rattle whoosh, the broom was thrust violently at her. Luckily, she had by then stepped back off the carpet of bones and had a firm footing, so she was able to jump backwards. *Un*luckily, that had the effect of jamming her between the tunnel wall and the rock. Her rump stuck fast. The harder she pushed back in an attempt to stay away from the broom, the more the back part of her body spread and the tighter it was held. She could have freed herself by going forwards, but by now the broom was upon her, and its nasty looking bristles were right in her face.

They were nasty looking because they were very sharp looking, and the closer they came the sharper they seemed. *Bristles* wasn't the best word for them, in fact. They were much more dangerous than bristles. They were more like enormous black needles. Any one of them could have gone right through her, and the nearest was now almost touching her. She could do nothing to get away from them.

'No Trespassing!'

The voice, as thin and sharp as one of the needles, came, strangely, from beneath the threatening bundle. Then she realised the bundle had a pair of short, thick legs keeping it a little way off the ground. The paws on the end of the legs, each with a set of long claws, were pointing away from her. So this was the back end of the animal, whatever kind of animal it was, and it had come at her in reverse. Where was the voice coming from, in that case? She had heard Dad Allen complain about people who talked through their backsides. Was that what this creature was doing?

She had no sooner begun to consider that than she saw a face with bright little eyes peering out at her from between what must be the animal's rear legs. How could that be? Had the animal doubled up under itself to look at her? If that were the case, though, its head would be upside down; and this head was the right way up. It was also much too small to be a match for the sizeable body above it.

'My Dad says *Go Away!*'

The sizeable body, then, must be Dad, and this narrow face belonged to a youngster who had crawled underneath his spiky parent to tell Sheena she was not welcome.

'Spickle! Come back here at once! Leave your father to do his job! He doesn't need you under his paws!'

This second voice had come from beyond the bristles. It was a mother speaking, Sheena surmised. Mum Allen could sound like that.

The sharp little nose and the bright little eyes moved backwards away from Sheena, then stopped. Sheena could still see the eyes gleaming through the longest of the needles.

'I'm stuck!' said the thin voice.

'Ouch!' came a third, deeper voice. 'You'd better get *un*stuck: you're sticking *me* with your *spines*!'

Spines! Spines! That was the word! And these must be porcuspines, Sheena decided.

Spickle had obviously got himself into a bit of a prickle. He had pushed his way forward under his father's stomach (uninvited, it sounded like) to deliver his warning. If he had little bristles at all like his father's big ones, they would be pointing backwards. The harder he tried to back out of the situation, the more painfully he would be jabbing his father in the stomach.

'Ouch! Stop moving! Ouch!'

Sheena felt safer, for the moment. Little Spickle was preventing his father from thrusting his spines at Sheena a second time. This was an opportunity for her to take more control: she had had enough of these sharp points threatening her very tender nose. She addressed the larger animal, although she had yet to see his face,

'Well, Mr. Porcuspine. This seems to be a case of the sticker stuck. What are you going to do about it? You're rather in my way, you know.'

'And you're rather in my den.'

'Well if you want me out of it, you'll have to move.'

'I can't.'

'And *I* can't.'

That was the young porcuspine speaking again: he didn't want to be forgotten. (There was another loud 'Ouch!' How could his father forget him?)

'Yes you can,' Sheena said. The mechanics of the situation were clear to her.

'You can both move forwards instead of backwards.'

'What, so that you can gobble up Spickle?'

This voice came from further back once more. The mother porcuspine had quickly realised that a move forward by either father or son would expose her precious infant to an animal she had not seen and whose voice she did not recognise. There might be danger here.

'Well please yourselves,' said Sheena, 'I'm in no hurry.'

She was beginning to be in a hurry, however. She had wasted too much time on these subterranean detours. All she wanted to do now was get back to where Pebble and Sandstepper were, say her goodbyes, and set off for the campsite.

She could hear the parent porcuspines talking to each other in low voices. Then the mother spoke again.

'Spickle, tell me what you can see.'

'Dad's tail.'

'What about through it?'

'Can't see through it.'

The large bundle of spines moved away from Sheena a little way, but not enough to uncover the youngster, just enough to let his bright little eyes appear once more, still between his father's rear legs.

'What about now?'

'I can see a serval cat; but it's not the usual colour, it's black and white like us.'

'I'm not a servile cat,' said Sheena, 'any more than I'm a mere cat. I'm a cat, that's all.'

'And we're not porcupines,' said the youngster,' we're porcu*pines*.

'We don't even *have* spines, we have quills.'

'But they're very sharp quills,' the mother added from behind all of this.

As if to emphasise her words, the male porcupine shook the back half of his body, and his quills rattled loudly.

'And they have barbs on the end,' she continued. 'If we stick just one in you, it will stay there, work its way deep into your flesh and make it fester and rot.

'So if you do anything to harm Spickle we'll make sure you leave here with something to remember us by. Otherwise we'll let you pass through peacefully. Which is it to be?'

'Peaceful passage please,' Sheena was quick to say.

'Alright; but we'll be watching very carefully…'

The male porcupine slowly moved away from Sheena, his topmost quills brushing the roof of the tunnel (sand came down). Spickle emerged into full view as his father disappeared round the corner.

In overall shape Spickle was not unlike a very small, very untidy honey badger, and that worried Sheena a bit: he might be small but his father was much larger. She was therefore happy to see no sign of big teeth, nor even of little ones that might be big one day. He was mainly covered in short bristles, with just a few slightly longer ones.

Spickle, it seemed, was quite ready to do something towards safeguarding his own future. As soon as he was out from under his father he turned quickly round so that his bristles, such as they were, pointed at Sheena. Then he raised them and backed towards her, threateningly, obviously trying them out for frightpower.

'We have very sharp quills!' he said menacingly.

Sheena counted the bristles that might qualify as quills. There were only half a dozen.

'Spickle, come here immediately!'

The male porcupine had been replaced by the female, facing

67

towards Sheena. She was almost as big as the male. She scrutinised Sheena carefully. She seemed satisfied that this strange animal (who had had kept her teeth and claws well out of sight) was no threat. She was, however, annoyed with Spickle.

Spickle realised that from the tone of her voice. He scuttled towards his mother, his spines subsiding.

'Mind your p's and q's,' his mother said. 'We have an agreement with this cat, whatever kind of cat it is.'

Sheena had always thought p's and q's were pleases and thanq-yous, but maybe they were prickles and quills. In either case her relationship with these porcupines was becoming more civilized.

Then she remembered the bones. Agreements were agreements but bones were bones. She needed to know more about these ones scattered along the floor of the tunnel. She deliberately, but as if by accident, kicked one so that it rattled against the others.

'Er…fond of bones, are you?'

'Oh, those!' said the female.

'Don't worry, we just collected those from hereabouts. We chew on them so that we can grow quills quickly. We need lots of replacements.'

'You mean you stick lots of quills into other animals?'

'No, no. They fall out very easily, that's all. Stop. Look.'

Spickle had by now disappeared beyond his father. The female had turned around and begun to lead Sheena down the tunnel, with Spickle and his father going on ahead. There were chambers to either side. Sheena paused at the female's command and peered into one. There were quills scattered across its floor. They looked like the pointed and painted sticks Thomas and Amy used in a game where you had to remove one stick at a time from a pile, without disturbing any of the others. (The game often ended up with Amy disturbing Thomas by pricking him with one of the sticks, or the other way round, and Mum Allen banning it for the rest of the week.)

'Come along then,' called the male from round the next bend.

'Let's get you to the outside, if that's where you want to be.'

'Come along,' called Spickle from even further ahead. It seems he had insisted on being at the front of this little procession. 'Let's get you outside.'

As she followed the porcupines through their living quarters and beyond into a wide, straight tunnel, Sheena noticed that the walls, previously sandy earth, were becoming stony. Before long she saw weak light ahead, strengthening as they approached what must be the entrance to the porcupines' den. The light continued to get brighter, and they eventually stopped in a larger, rocky chamber – more a small cave, really. Sunshine poured in across the floor from a low entrance.

'All of this started off at the other end as a meerkats' burrow,' Sheena said. 'Is this place yours or theirs?'

'Theirs, really, but we have an agreement with them,' said Spickle's father.

Agreements obviously played a large part in the porcupines' lives.

'They dug it, but it's too far from Deepden Mound for them to easily guard it; so they allow us to live here as long as we stop other animals coming in.'

'Or in your case, out,' added the female. 'There's no clause in the agreement about stopping animals leaving, but when we heard you coming and realised you were not a meerkat we decided we should block the tunnel just in case.

'But you look harmless enough. Why are you here?'

'I'm here because I'm trying to be somewhere else. I'm lost.

Can you show me where Deepden is? On the outside, I mean: I've had enough of the inside.'

'This *is* Deepden. It's all connected. If you mean Deepden Mound, the centre of the system, we can show you where that is easily enough. This way.'

'This way!' said Spickle with an extra bit of punctuation.

They emerged from the cave into bright sunshine, and Sheena had to narrow her eyes to see. They had come out between two large boulders at the foot of a high mound of rocks and sand, covered in dusty shrubs. Spickle did not hesitate but led the way up among the rocks towards their highest point.

The flat top of the little hill was bare of vegetation, so that when they were all standing there they could see clearly in every direction. The sun was high in the sky and it was very hot.

'Over there.'

The male porcupine was looking at a point in the distance.

'Over there!' said Spickle, alongside his father and looking the same way.

A long way off, half-way to the horizon it seemed, there was a sandy mound. The other, lower mounds that surrounded it were hardly visible. Had she really come so far? Had this whole landscape been tunnelled under so that it held a great network of passages and chambers? That would explain why she had got lost so easily; and it made her realise she shouldn't venture down there again unescorted.

'Thank you very much. I need to leave now.'

'Wait. It's a long, dry journey back to Deepden. Try some of these first.'

The female porcupine stepped down from the flat rock and nosed among the bushes. There were some small berries lying on the ground and she rolled a few out into the open with her snout. She took one in her mouth and bit into it, and a sharp, slightly sweet smell filled the air.

Sheena was not an eater of berries, nor of any fruit in fact; but she was thirsty again, and didn't think she would have much success if she scratched down into this stony earth to find grubs or other wrigglies. So she too stepped down from the rock, took a berry in her mouth, and bit into it.

It did not hold very much liquid, so she had to crunch and chew it, and was left with a mouthful of dry fibres which she then had difficulty swallowing. She knew there must be some goodness in the berries, though, so she made herself chew and swallow several more.

'I'm Nungu, by the way,' the female said.

'So am I,' said Spickle's father, who had stayed up on top. 'Together we're Nungunungu.'

'And I'm Spickle, but when I'm a bit bigger I'll be Nungu as well. Then we'll be Nungunungunungu.'

Sheena wondered how a large porcupine family would use their names without spending a lot of time over it.

'Dad, look over there!'

Spickle had stayed with his father. They were now peering towards the horizon on the side away from Deepden Mound, where, in the distance, there was a line of dark vegetation stretching across the landscape as far as the eye could see

'Well, now, you might be interested in this, since you're interested in meerkats' (father).

'You might be interested in this!' (son).

Sheena jumped up alongside them once more. A single animal was coming towards them across the dusty plain, from the direction of the line of trees. It was a meerkat.

As the animal drew closer, it became clear that it was hurt. It was moving slowly on all fours, and stumbling, and there were dark patches on its body that might well be blood. Twice it stopped, and its head drooped to the ground. It was obviously trying to reach the hill on which they were standing.

The adult porcupines and Sheena wound their way down through the boulders. Spickle did it in his own way. He curled himself up into a ball and set off rolling down the track.

'Spickle!' His mother called out too late to stop him. By then his ears were well tucked away between his paws. He came straight for Sheena, and she had to jump to one side to avoid being perforated. His stiff little bristles protected him fully, so it did not matter that he bounced from one rock to another on the way down. Bouncing off things seemed to be part of the fun.

At the bottom of the hill he bumped solidly into a large rock directly in his path, and rebounded several feet. He uncurled and shook himself, making a little rattling noise like a junior version of his father's.

His parents and Sheena arrived at the bottom of the mound just as the meerkat reached the beginning of the short trail leading to the cave entrance. Sheena thought she recognised him through the dust and blood on his fur. It was the small, dark meerkat that had jumped down and run away as Nyegere approached Deepden Mound.

The meerkat peered at them through half-closed eyes, then spoke weakly.

'They will come tonight!' he said.

He did not seem to know who or what he was talking to. He was close to unconsciousness. Did he know who or what he was talking *about*?

'Who will come?' Sheena asked.

'The Utongo.'

Chapter Eight: Mtego

Going in
You think there's a way out;
Turning round
You find there's not.

Sheena would take a warning back to Deepden, alone. The injured meerkat (who Sheena would find out later was called Shuffle, since even when he was not injured he had a strange, flat-footed way of walking) needed to rest here with the porcupines. The porcupines themselves would have taken too long to cover that distance.

That's what they said, at least. There was another reason, however, why they were very reluctant to become involved; and that soon became plain.

'In any case,' said Nungu (the female Nungu), 'taking warnings is none of our business. Our business is to guard this entrance, that's all, for whoever we have an agreement with.'

She was obviously the more political of the pair of adults. Sheena guessed she was thinking that even if the Duwara of Deepden were warned, they might be overrun by the invading Utongo. Then what would happen to the agreement the porcupines had? They might be driven out of their comfortable den by the Utongo, as a punishment for helping the Duwara. It would be better to sit on the fence (or in the hole) until matters were settled one way or the other. Sheena was able to take a straight line across the hard ground, towards the distant mounds now beginning to cast afternoon shadows across the ground. Her decision had been straightforward too. Deepden Mound was back towards the campsite, so she would hardly need to go out of her way.

She had become attached to the strange animals who lived in Deepden. She liked their closeness (even if they did sleep so closely together, and so deeply, that they widdled on each other). She liked their assumption that help would be given when help was needed, and their readiness to give help themselves. She had enjoyed their morning ritual and their delight in the early sunshine, and had felt what it was like to share in the strength the sun gave them. She had become, briefly, a part of something bigger than herself, which for a cat was an unusual experience.

She had also been drawn to the individuals she had met. In particular she felt bound to Pebble: to save a life is to become a part of it.

Deepden too would be saved, if she had anything to do with it.

She had more to do with it than she expected.

It was Tuft who took the lead in asking her questions when she reached Deepden Mound. Moon, who was also there, listened carefully. So did another, older meerkat, whom Sheena had not seen before. His fur was graying, and the long claws on his front paws were very curved and lay across each other in different directions, loosely, as if they might fall out at any time. 'Crossclaw!' Sheena thought. From what Sandstepper had said it seemed he was a kind of Senior Tutor, the oldest and perhaps wisest of the Duwara.

Most of the meerkats had been resting in the cool underground chambers when she arrived, but came running out on all sides of her when the lookout barked.

Sheena told them what she knew from the little that Shuffle had been able to get out before he finally lost consciousness; and Tuft and Moon were able to explain, later, some of the things she did not understand.

Shuffle had decided to switch tribes, to leave the Duwara and join the Utongo. (Sheena's listeners were not surprised to hear that: they had suspected him for some time of considering such a move.) The arrival of Nyegere had spurred him into action, and he had jumped down and run off towards the Utongo homelands.

He had met the band of Utongo well past the porcupines' burrow, just where the plain disappeared into the line of trees, Sheena told them.

'That is not the porcupines' burrow, it is ours.' Crossclaw spoke for the first time, coldly.

'Duwara dug it out many generations ago. We allow the porcupines to live there so that we cannot be attacked through that entrance. It is the nearest part of the system to Longburrow, where the Utongo live.

'We call it Rockhome. It used to be where the Breeders went to give birth to their pups, until it became unsafe.'

The Utongo had mobbed Shuffle and savaged him. Their leader had also taunted him with their plans to attack Deepden, clearly intending that they should kill him, or at least injure him so badly that he would not be able to reach Deepden to give any warnings. He had escaped only because a hawk eagle had suddenly swept above them on its broad wings, and the Utongo had scattered under its shadow.

'Are you sure he said they are coming *tonight*?' Tuft asked. 'I can hardly believe that. Meerkats sleep at night.

'If it is true, however, we have a problem. We can scent-mark our boundaries, but that will not be enough to keep the Utongo away if they are determined to invade. There are not enough of us to guard every entrance to Deepden. The system was built many years ago when there were far more of us. The Utongo will be able to find a way in under cover of darkness. We will not know where they have entered, and we may be trapped. They are fierce fighters; and we have pups and injured meerkats to protect.'

'We could collapse some of the entrances.'

Another meerkat had spoken. He was short and strong-looking with bushy eyebrows and one claw on each front paw much longer than the others.

'That would take too long, Stab; and the Utongo could dig through anyway.'

It was in the nature of Sheena (you may have noticed) that whenever there was a Problem, a Plan came to her. It happened again now.

She could not help herself. 'I have a Plan,' she said.

In fact she had *had* a Plan, until this moment, to go straight on from here to the campsite and spend the rest of the week much nearer the family. She had done more hard travelling across this bare landscape (both on and under) than she had ever intended. A bit of drifting around would be nice for a change, she had thought.

The situation had changed around her, however.

'You will need to work out the details yourselves. You know Deepden. All I can do is give you an idea.'

She gave it to them. Tuft, Moon and the other meerkats listened intently.

'That might work,' said Tuft.

The meerkats discussed it. They discussed it at great length, until Sheena felt she had to prod them a bit.

'It will not work entirely. No plan is perfect; but this one will help...if you don't waste any more time.'

They didn't. Fifteen or so of the meerkats set off immediately for Rockhome and the porcupines' den. They were led by Stab. They would travel there by way of the tunnel system, partly to stay out of the heat of the mid-day sun, partly to avoid watchful eyes. Each one had precise instructions about what to do after that.

The remaining meerkats could only wait, and talk. Sheena would have liked to visit Pebble and Sandstepper straight away, but Tuft and Moon wanted her to hear more about the Duwara and their troubles. They seemed eager to share the burden of their leadership, as if they hoped this strange creature from a world elsewhere might be able to give them a new view of theirs.

Crossclaw listened carefully throughout, perhaps to make sure the story was told properly; but he did not say anything until near the end.

Shuffle was by no means the first Duwara meerkat to want to join the Utongo. The Utongo had not always been so cruel. Moving from one tribe to another had been quite an easy thing to do in years gone by, and it happened just as often the other way round. Young males from one group who had little chance of rising through the ranks to the point where they would be able to take a female and produce pups could choose to go off to find a female from the other group and mate with her. Both tribes were usually tolerant of that, even though only the number one male and female were supposed to have offspring.

'Why only them?' Sheena had asked.

'So that we have no more than one lot of pups to look after at a time,' said Moon. 'We all share in looking after them and bringing them up. That's quite difficult, because we have to spend so much time away from the burrow looking for food. So we must keep the number of pups down.'

'Why, then, did you ever allow young Utongo males to come and mate with your other females – even if it *was* 'unofficial'?'

'To bring fresh blood to the tribe. That's important.'

'We had to stop it, though,' said Tuft.

'Too many Utongo males were coming. We decided it was a plot. We had too many of their pups and had to spend too much time looking after them. There were also too many Utongo males living here. Soon we would have forgotten who we are. We would have become more Utongo than Duwara.

'So we began to place limits. Only one Utongo male could come at a time, and he could have only one litter with a Duwara female. After that, if he wanted to stay, he had to become just a Helper.

'The Utongo retaliated by making similar rules for our young males. Then there were squabbles about whether the rules were being broken, and the two tribes gradually became more suspicious of each other.

'A few months ago two foraging groups met in The Gorge and a major fight broke out. Meerkats were killed on both sides.'

The Gorge, he explained, lay between Rockhome and Longburrow, and was marked by the line of vegetation Sheena had seen from the top of the porcupines' hill. It was a long, deep cleft in the earth, a valley really, filled with trees and bushes, and a very good place to find food. It ran roughly from East to West: the sun came up at one end and followed its line over the course of the day.

'Since then we have been at war. Both tribes now lay claim to The Gorge, and there have been many skirmishes.

'We have never attacked one another's home burrows. But we have always expected that it would happen one day.

'We never thought it would happen one night, however.'

Now, at last, the agèd Crossclaw spoke again. His voice was not strong, but his words were.

'That kind of deceit is what we have come to expect from the

Utongo. They are no longer meerkats like us. And we must not become like *them*. They should be free to live under their sun; but we do not want them under ours.'

The injury to Sandstepper's leg was much improved. He had rested, and been fed, and was ready to go to the surface to help with the defence of Deepden. Pebble, however, was still too weak to leave the burrow. When Sheena arrived the pair of them were lying in the outer chamber.

Sheena heard Fara's voice coming from the smaller chamber, where Pebble and Sandstepper had rested overnight.

'When the day has become cooler we will...' she said.

She was busy brushing flat with her tail the sand the two meerkats had been lying on, rather as if she was making a hospital bed. She didn't finish the task, but came out past where they all were and drifted off down one of the tunnels, leaving the sand on one side of the chamber floor still unswept.

Sheena told Pebble and Sandstepper all that had happened since she got lost in the tunnels. When they heard her latest Plan, they were impressed.

'We want to be there when it all happens!' said Pebble, excitedly.

'That's the whole point,' said Sheena. 'You can't be. There aren't enough of you to go round. This is *instead* of you.'

Sheena and Sandstepper were on top of the mound when the Duwara meerkats began to arrive back at the main mound. It was late in the afternoon, and the sun was well down in the sky. Most had travelled underground, and emerged one by one from nearby exits. They had all been very busy, it seemed, since their return earlier from Rockhome.

Tuft and Moon were there also, but Crossclaw was not. Tuft decided he and Moon would visit a nearby tunnel entrance to see what had been accomplished. Sheena went with them to find out whether her instructions had been carefully carried out. Sandstepper went along too: it was now clear that he was a meerkat of some rank.

They travelled above ground, and soon reached their destination – one of the outlying mounds. It had a double entrance, Sheena saw as they came close, tucked away at the base of a low sand cliff atop of which stood a line of bushes: there were two tunnels a few yards apart.

The two meerkats whose job it had been to come to this spot earlier had also returned with the inspection party.

'Careful!' one of them said.

Tuft went into the left-hand tunnel, but stopped just out of sight then backed out.

'Very good!' he said. 'I wouldn't want to run in there even during the daytime.'

Sheena knew why, but she went into the tunnel to see for herself.

A little way inside the entrance there were several porcupine quills jammed into the floor and pointing at an angle towards the entrance. They had been driven into the sandy earth. Any animal rushing in at night would impale itself horribly. Here was a tunnel that need not be guarded. Sheena's suggestion had been that any entrance the meerkats thought they could not defend should be booby-trapped just like this. An attacker would receive a very pointed message.

Things were arranged differently in the other tunnel of the pair. Sheena had learnt something from Spickle's entanglement with his father. There were quills set into its floor too, but also into its walls. These quills, like those in the other tunnel, were at an angle, but this time pointed away from the entrance. A meerkat charging in here would be able to brush past the quills with no difficulty; but if he tried to get out again in a hurry…

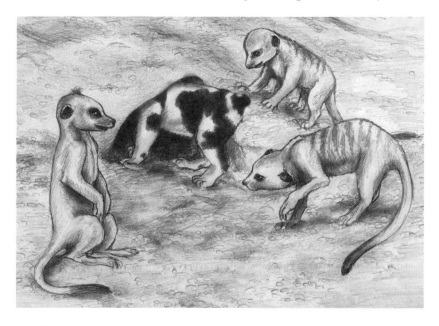

The idea was that some entrances, like this second one, should be guarded inside, beyond the inward-pointing quills, by the biggest and bravest of the Duwara males (and by some females – a few of *them* were bigger and braver than some of the males). An invader would be allowed past the trap, then suddenly and ferociously attacked so that he was driven backwards onto the dreadful points. Each of those little battles would be quickly won, it was hoped; and the impaled intruder would block the entrance for any Utongo behind him.

The younger and more timid meerkats would help where they could.

By the time they returned to Deepden Mound nearly all of the meerkats who had been sent to collect quills and set them in place had reported back. Last to arrive, some time after all of the others, was Stab.

'It is all done,' he said to Tuft.

Tuft, and Moon (who had a say in such matters), gave everyone final orders. The whole tribe then went a little way towards the slope and did some final foraging for the day. Since they were all scratching, sniffing and digging in the same small area, it was unlikely they would feed well; but it seemed to matter to them that they should have this last feast together. Not very much chirruping went on.

Tuft and Moon returned to Deepden Mound with a small group of meerkats that included Sandstepper. They would defend the heart of the system, if any Utongo got that far. All of the others, the ones who would position themselves near the end of outlying tunnels, departed in ones and twos and in many different directions. They would fight their own battles in the tight darkness, and see each other again only when it was all over – if they survived.

The sun was nearing the horizon by the time Sheena and the others reached the Mound.

'Would you like to see the Nursery?' Moon asked Sheena. 'It's not too far, and the tunnel to it is quite wide.' It seemed she wanted to take her mind off the fearful battle that lay ahead.

She led the way down a tunnel that descended sharply from a fork not far inside the main entrance. It narrowed a little, and other tunnels fed into it before it ended in a small chamber with dry grass on the floor. A meerkat was lying in the centre of the chamber. Three very young meerkat pups were nuzzling at her stomach. It was obviously feeding time.

'They're nearly finished; they'll be asleep soon,' said the nursing meerkat.

'A slurp then a sleep,' Sheena thought. 'Not a bad life.'

Then, puzzled, she spoke to Moon.

'I thought *you* were the mother of the litter.'

'I am; but other female meerkats feed them. That means I can go out foraging more often, and build up my strength so that I can have more babies soon.

'Tuft and I are the biggest and healthiest male and female, you see. That's another reason why we produce most of the pups, to keep the tribe strong. We have to keep ourselves ready for that task.

'We all have a part to play in the daily life of the Duwara. Some of us are nurses, like Thornpaw here; some of us are teachers like Sandstepper; then some of us are given the job of bringing back food for the pups when they begin to eat properly. Tuft and I are the Breeders; and we all take turns at sentry duty.'

Dad Allen taught Economics to older students at the school Amy and Thomas went to. He was very interested in his subject, so Thomas sometimes had to listen to Economics lessons delivered round the Allens' dining room table. Sheena sometimes *chose* to listen, and she knew that what Moon had just described was called the Principle of Division of Labour. That was not much more than words to her, however: cats did everything for themselves, apart from an occasional bit of reciprocal licking.

'Do you all fight?'

'We will if we have to, to defend the burrow, to defend the pups, to defend our way of life. We'd rather just frighten other animals away, though, by making our great big fuss.'

She was talking about the war dance.

'That doesn't work on other meerkats, however: they know it's all show.

'If the Utongo do come at night, we'd be dancing in the dark and wasting our time anyway. There will be no way of putting them off, and the fighting will be very real.'

This was such a peaceful scene, down in the nursery chamber, that Sheena felt a temporary calm descend on her, and would have liked to stay longer. The pups were just beginning to look like meerkats, and already had a light covering of fur. Their eyes were closed. That could be because they were concentrating on sucking, or because they were nearly asleep, or even perhaps because they had yet to open them for the first time. They reminded her of the kittens she herself had never had (if it's possible to be reminded of something that hasn't happened to you).

Then they reminded her that something bad was about to take place unless she and the adult meerkats were able to stop it. She and Moon left the chamber and returned to the surface.

By now it was dark. Unfortunately (but perhaps not by accident) it was a moonless night. Even Sheena could not see far across the plain, and she knew the meerkats' night vision was not as good as hers. They would be able to tell what was going on more by sound and smell than by sight, until the Utongo got very close, too close.

Despite the preparations the Duwara had made, there were many unknowns in the situation. Who could guess how many Utongo would attack? Which entrances would they try to enter by? How successful would the booby traps prove? How determined would the Utongo be, even if the traps worked well? Which of the Duwara might die in the battle?

Mtego

Would the Utongo even come?

Chapter Nine: Ushindi

Something won,
Something lost,
Never complete:
There's always a cost.

They did come. They came silently to begin with.

Tuft and Moon had asked Sheena to stay on the mound with them, since her night vision *was* so much better. Crossclaw was also there. They had decided that they would have a clearer sense of what was happening across the whole Deepden system if they stayed in the open and up high, where any noise from even the more distant entrances would come to them on the night air.

They settled down to wait. Sheena's sharp ears picked up slight sounds from across the plain – the scuffle of a stone, a soft hiss, a click of what might be teeth; but she could see almost nothing in the distant darkness. The Duwara with her were sniffing the air; but there was no breeze to bring the smell of other meerkats to them. They waited more.

The first yelp came from quite close at hand, and startled them all. The yelp was followed by snarling, hissing and spitting, then by more yelps.

It was impossible to tell which meerkats had been hurt in this first encounter, or even if it had been an encounter between meerkat and meerkat or meerkat and quill.

More yelps drifted in from further afield, and some screams, and lots of snarling. Once Sheena thought she heard Stab calling in the distance, but his call was not repeated. There was the sound of animal claws scuttering in the sand, not very far away but growing fainter. Then they seemed to get nearer again, and increase in number.

The Duwara meerkats had been told to stay in the tunnels, and not come out into the open where they might be outnumbered; so all of the running around that now seemed to take place in the darkness must be by Utongo. The Duwara on the Mound expected to have to jump down at any moment and take refuge in the main tunnel, and then perhaps to have to turn and defend it.

There was silence again, for some time, and Sheena strained her ears to catch any patter of paws coming close once more.

Then there was a terrible screaming from some distance away.

Then silence again.

What was happening?

They could not know; and that pattern – of sudden cries of pain, sounds of struggle, sudden silence – continued through the night. No direct attack was made against the Mound itself.

As dawn approached the silences between cries became longer. Soon they would know what the cost of defending Deepden had been.

When the sky lightened along the horizon, Tuft and Moon decided the attack was over. There had been no sounds of conflict for a long time; and as the light strengthened they could see no signs of Utongo.

Tuft gave a series of high yelps. They were echoed by yelps coming from some distance around the mound, where the other entrances were. They were not replies however, Sheena realised, they were relays: Tuft's call was being passed on, and on again, out to the furthest outposts of the Deepden system.

Soon the rest of the tribe began to arrive. They came in ones and twos, some helping others, some crawling weakly, others quite jaunty and excited. Stab arrived walking strongly. The only injury he had was a deep scratch near one eye.

They all had different stories to tell, and most began to tell them immediately they reached the sandy space around the mound.

'I didn't know they were there until…'

'Did you see…?'

'There were three of them…'

'It's a good job…'

'He won't come back in a hurry…'

Some of the meerkats were silent, however, as if what they had seen and done had affected them deeply.

Tuft tried to keep some order, but it was difficult.

Then the sun began to show over the hard, dark line of the horizon, and that was the signal for the meerkats who had returned to jump up onto one or other of the mounds and prepare to greet the new day. Even those who were injured managed to scramble up, some with help, to be with the rest of the tribe at Sunwake.

They all fell silent on their separate mounds as the sun rose; and they stood there facing it with their heads erect, their sharp faces pointing forwards and their paws held in front of them – less like rows of tennis spectators, now, than like small choirs (Sheena thought), each waiting for its choirmaster to raise his baton; then they would lift their sheets of music, and begin.

The pale sunlight glinted in their eyes; but it also gleamed on the bloodstains running down the fur of some of the more badly hurt. The Ndugu would soon be busy.

The effect of the strengthening sunlight was extraordinary. The excited meerkats became calm, the silent ones lifted their heads, the injured ones stood straighter.

They stayed up on the mounds for a long time, even though they were obviously very tired: they were unused to being awake through the night, and certainly unused to fighting such prolonged battles. Eventually the young meerkat Sheena remembered falling backwards the morning before fell backwards again. This time he did not get up, but just lay there on the sand, fast asleep already.

Then the meerkats jumped down onto the hard earth in front of their mounds and began to greet each other – sniffing, rubbing, licking and embracing. Today, however, the greetings seemed more subdued; and the young meerkats did not play.

One or two stragglers arrived and they all headed into the

burrow, by one entrance or another. There would be time for their stories later.

Only Tuft, Moon and Crossclaw stayed outside with Sheena. It was too early to tell whether or not the defence of Deepden had been what might be called a victory. Not all of the meerkats had returned yet, and that worried the two leaders.

'This would have been a terrible night in the history of the Duwara, if you had not helped us,' said Crossclaw.

It was terrible enough, in its own way. Just then Stab burst out of the main entrance and turned quickly to face them.

'The pups have been taken! Pebble has been taken!' he said.

Chapter Ten: Chemba

The same as go back
But not quite defeat.
Both cowardly and wise,
My name is ……..

The meerkat who had been looking after the pups had been badly injured. Both her ears were torn and there were deep gouges in her side where claws had raked through her flesh. She had tried to resist but had been thrown back against the chamber wall by a rush of Utongo against her. She was still unconscious when she was found.

Pebble had been alone in his chamber, which was not far from the nursery, so there was no way of being certain what had happened to him. The sand in the chamber was churned up and sprinkled with spots of blood: it seemed he too had fought, as much as he was able. Then he must have been made to leave with the Utongo raiding party; or perhaps he had just bravely followed the meerkats who had picked up the pups in their mouths and carried them off.

Where to? All the Duwara could do was follow the tracks.

Perhaps the Utongo had found their way here, to the heart of Deepden, by chance (but by which entrance had they broken into the system?) Perhaps, however, this raid on the nursery had been planned from the beginning, and all of the other attacks on all of

93

the other entrances had been a diversion. If the Utongo had been clever enough to develop a plan like that, perhaps they were clever enough not to have headed straight back towards Longburrow.

Tuft directed matters. The meerkats were all very tired. Some were quite badly hurt. It would have made no sense for the whole tribe to go chasing off, blindly, perhaps to meet a superior force of Utongo either in the tunnels or outside on the plain. The females were needed to help look after the injured (it seemed that all female meerkats were Ndugu when they needed to be). So only four of the stronger males set off with Tuft, following the marks in the sand and the bitter smell of Utongo in the dank air of the labyrinth.

Tuft decided there should be a second group, however, travelling on the surface. They would know which way to go by listening to the sounds Tuft and his companions made as they followed the trail through the tunnels: their hearing was quite sharp enough for that, and in addition they would be able to pick up through their paws the vibrations caused by the other group's paws several feet beneath them. If they needed to signal downwards they could do so by thumping the ground.

This second group, led by Sandstepper, would be able to see what was happening out on the plain; and both groups could meet up whenever the underground trackers came near an entrance. If the Utongo were carrying the pups, that would slow them down, and one or other of the pursuing Duwara groups might well catch up with them.

Sheena would go with Sandstepper. There was no question, now, of her simply leaving and heading back to the campsite. She was beginning to feel that her Plan, of which she had been so proud, had given the Duwara too much confidence. They had not taken the care they might have done to protect the heart of Deepden. They should have had guards near the nursery at least. If she could help more, and more carefully, she would.

There was soon no doubt as to which way the Utongo had made their escape. Sandstepper led the way swiftly across the plain, stopping only occasionally to listen to the faint sounds coming from under the earth. It seemed that Tuft was having no difficulty in following the trail; and the trail led straight towards The Gorge.

Not only that: it led straight towards Rockhome.

If the Utongo had left through there, did that mean they had also entered through there? Had they attacked the porcupines and driven them out of the tunnels, or dug round them? Or had the porcupines simply let them through?

When Tuft and his group arrived at the Rockhome chambers, by the same long, straight tunnel that had taken Sheena to them, they were open and unprotected to comers and goers alike. The strong scent of Utongo indicated that the raiders had been there, but it was difficult to tell how long before.

The porcupines were at home; but they were not at home to callers. The meerkats found one of the chamber entrances wholly blocked by porcupine bristles, attached to porcupine – father porcupine by the look of it.

Sandstepper's group arrived at the entrance to Rockhome soon after, and Tuft sent for Sheena: she had had the most recent dealings with Nungunungu.

They could get no response from Nungu. Was he dead? No: when Tuft patted his bristles sideways with a careful paw, rattling them, they bristled (as bristles do), then rattled back. That was all. Nungu would not turn, or speak; and they could not tell if the other two porcupines, mother and Spickle, were in the chamber

with him. Had *they* been killed, perhaps, and was Nungu injured
or in shock?

They could not wait to find out. Their further questions to his
spiny back went unanswered, and they decided they must just
move on.

Tuft reported all of that to Sandstepper and the other group,
who had not entered the outer cave. They had instead climbed up
through the vegetation to the rocky outcrop, in order to survey
the landscape ahead. There were no Utongo in view.

All the Duwara could do now was press on towards The
Gorge, and perhaps Longburrow beyond that; but the trail
outside Rockhome was cold. The hard earth had retained no
imprints that could be identified as Utongo, and the early
morning breeze must have carried away whatever smell the
invaders had left behind.

It was some distance from Rockhome to The Gorge, much

further than it had looked to Sheena from the top of the hill the day before. She herself was tired, and the pace of the two groups, now combined, had slowed.

As they came close to the dark line of vegetation Sheena was aware for the first time of how dense it was. In this generally dry part of the Park these trees and bushes were growing strongly together, casting dark shadows on the earth beneath. Sandstepper explained that there was water in the bottom of The Gorge for most of the year, and even when it dried up, as it had recently done, the earth held enough moisture, deep down, to keep the plants alive, if only just. Then when the rains came and water poured into The Gorge once more, the growing recommenced, the trees spread their leaves wide and the bushes became luxuriant again.

There were always worms and grubs to be found in The Gorge's rich earth, whatever the time of year.

That, however, was as near as they got to The Gorge. Suddenly there was a rustling at several points along the edge of the vegetation, and three separate groups of meerkats sprang into the open.

'Utongo!' said Sandstepper; and the Duwara halted. Every one of the three groups outnumbered them.

Numbers were not everything, however. Sheena could see even from here that some of the Utongo were injured and were having difficulty standing in a fully upright posture; and there were bloodstains to be seen on several coats. They too had paid a price for the attack of the night before.

Sheena expected them to begin their meerkat wardance; but they did not. Instead, they dropped onto all fours and began to move forward in what was in fact a more threatening way. If the Duwara stayed where they were they would soon be outflanked, and would have difficulty escaping.

Neither side made a sound: there was only a bitter silence.

There was no sign of either the pups or Pebble; and now the Duwara could not go forward, must retreat before it was too late. It seemed the Utongo had claimed The Gorge as theirs.

The journey back to Deepden was wearisome. The Utongo meerkats had not followed them when they turned away from The Gorge, but had stayed in the open a long time, watching. Sheena and the Duwara meerkats travelled slowly across the open ground, and it was the middle of the day by the time they reached Deepden Mound. If only they had decided to use the tunnels, and had gone back by way of Rockhome, things might have been different.

Chapter Eleven: Tishio

Both more and less than a treat;
Knot the end of the thread;
If it's carried out
You may end up dead.

They might have discovered that the pups and Pebble were in Rockhome all the time, in a porcupine chamber, trapped there by porcupine quills, guarded by Utongo, and either slashed (in Pebble's case) or smothered (in the case of the pups) into silence. They were not the only Duwara held prisoner there, either.

The Utongo raiding party had realised from the sounds behind them in the tunnels that they were being pursued at high speed, and would soon be caught. They could have dropped the pups and abandoned Pebble, which would have allowed them to run more quickly; but they could hear sounds of pursuit overhead also (although further back), and feared they might be overtaken above. So when they got to Rockhome they took refuge in the largest of the porcupine chambers. Just how they were able to do that became clear later in the day.

Back in Deepden, the Duwara rested and recovered through the afternoon. The wounded were treated by the Ndugu. By early evening most of the tribe were stirring again: they had not eaten since morning, and needed to go out foraging before nightfall.

Tuft did not think the Utongo would come again that night.

'They have their own wounds to recover from. They did not chase us when we turned back from The Gorge.

'Besides, it is possible they got all they came for, last night.'

'But why would they come for the pups?' asked Moon. 'And what use could Pebble be to them?'

Those questions could not be answered for the moment.

The Duwara had just returned from eating, and the sun was nearing the horizon. Sheena had gone with them, and Sandstepper had helped her find some crunchy beetles by digging under an unusually light-coloured bush near the top of the slope.

She caught up with Crossclaw as they came back to the main Deepden entrance: he could move only slowly on his old, thin limbs. Fara was just in front of him, and Sheena wondered whether she had been helping him to find food.

Sheena had half-expected the meerkats to jump up onto the mound for an evening ritual, but they did not.

'Why don't you all climb on the mound at the end of the day, to watch the sun go down?' she asked Crossclaw. 'You watch it rise every morning.'

(Dad Allen was very fond of sitting outside, wherever he was, and enjoying the sunset, particularly with a glass in his hand. Sheena wondered briefly whether he was doing it now, not so very far away. Were Thomas and Amy with him?)

There was a pause before Crossclaw replied, as if he had not known she was there, and needed to re-focus his mind on the present.

'We have no need to. It is with us from morning to night. We know it is there, throughout, and we feel safe in its presence.

'Each morning, though, we must renew. That is why we have

Sunwake. We must make sure that the sun has returned to us; and we must let it give us some of its strength, and remind us of who we are.'

Sheena was still puzzled by what Tuft had said the day before, about the Utongo living under a different sun. This idea of two suns was altogether strange to Sheena, who had thought there was only one. She said as much.

'You would know the truth if you visited Longburrow. To get there you must go down into The Gorge, and leave our sun, the True Sun, behind. There is no sun above The Gorge. When you have climbed the further side and come out from under the trees, you are in a different place and under a different sun – the Utongo sun.'

That didn't really tell Sheena much more than Tuft had done previously, but she had no time to ask further questions. One meerkat had as usual climbed onto the mound to act as look-out, and now barked sharply. He was staring in the direction of Rockhome. Other meerkats jumped up, and lined up, alongside him.

There was a solitary meerkat in the distance, coming towards them. Sheena recognised him immediately, since he was walking in the same slow, stumbling manner as when he arrived at Rockhome from the direction of The Gorge. It was Shuffle, who had tried to join the Utongo and been savaged by them.

He came closer, very slowly. He was in even worse condition than when she had last seen him. Some of the blood on his fur was fresh, trickling down from several open gashes on his chest and legs. The base of his tail was very badly chewed. One eye was closed and swollen, and one ear was missing altogether.

He had taken the whole afternoon and more to reach Deepden, travelling on the surface in the hope that Duwara meerkats, out foraging, might see him and offer him help.

It was from him that they learned much of what happened when the small Utongo raiding party – only six or so of them – arrived at Rockhome.

They had in fact come there twice, once on their way to Deepden and once, as was already known, on their way back with the pups and Pebble.

On the first occasion the porcupines had done what they were supposed to do as part of their agreement with the Duwara: they had blocked the tunnels...at least to begin with. The Utongo had then, however, done much talking. Shuffle, as soon as he recognised harsh Utongo voices, had stayed out of sight in a corner of the small chamber in which he had been resting.

He could hear only parts of the discussion taking place in the main tunnel; but it soon became clear that the Utongo were trying to persuade Nungunungu to let them through – he caught phrases like 'the rest of our attacking force', 'when we have defeated them,' 'a new agreement', and 'live here forever'. Were they trying to buy their way into Deepden with promises?

They were; and Sheena was disappointed to learn that they had succeeded. The porcupines had decided to change allegiances, had lowered their spines and stepped aside into one of their other chambers to allow the Utongo to pass. So much for their agreement with the Duwara.

'I might have expected as much from animals who fight backwards in that cowardly way,' she thought. 'You should never stand behind a porcupine for two reasons,' she decided. 'The second one is because you can't rely on him to stand behind *you*.'

Parents sometimes did strange things, however, when an offspring's future was involved.

The porcupines would by now have regretted their decision.

Sheena realised that as Shuffle told the second part of his story.

They helped him down into the burrow first. The evening was cooling quickly, and he was beginning to shiver – through fatigue and shock as much as through cold, and also through some relief at being back where he now knew he belonged.

Some of the Ndugu ministered to him in the chamber where Pebble and Sandstepper had rested, giving him morsels to eat, licking his wounds, lying down next to him to warm him.

He struggled to get through the rest of his tale. He seemed to have something to tell, beyond the events themselves, that the Duwara should know.

The porcupines had ignored him after the Utongo left to go further into Deepden. Shuffle decided it was because they were ashamed of their treachery. He considered trying to get to Deepden before the Utongo, travelling on the surface, so that he could warn the Duwara about this underground, underhand attack; but his injuries would slow him down too much, he knew. So he lay there, listening to the muffled sound of the porcupines talking but unable to do more than guess at what they were saying. He was there for a long time, in some pain and drifting in and out of consciousness.

After what seemed a very long time he heard the Utongo returning hurriedly from the main Deepden system, arguing among themselves as they ran. Lying very still, he watched them pass the chamber entrance. He was horrified to see that three of them had small, furry bodies swinging from their mouths. He was equally horrified to see a young meerkat stumbling along near the end of the group, harassed by a much larger meerkat nipping at his ankles with sharp teeth.

'That's Pebble!' he realised.

Then he was horrified on his own behalf. The meerkats and

the porcupines met once more, and talked once more. Suddenly there was a scrabbling outside the chamber entrance. Two meerkats rushed in and stood over him, teeth bared and claws at the ready. The porcupines had committed another betrayal.

'So, Shuffler! This is where you escaped to!'

He had told them his name when they confronted him the first time. 'Shuffler' was meant to be insulting.

What they did to him next was meant to be damaging. They attacked him viciously, as if they were continuing the beating they had begun the day before. He was saved only by the fact that they were in a great hurry.

'Up! Up! Move! Go!'

They forced him to rise, and bundled him into the tunnel and then along it until they reached the largest of the porcupine chambers. The other Utongo meerkats were already there. So were the pups, lying together in a sad little heap in one corner. So was Pebble, lying in a frightened and angry little heap in another. So were Nungunungu. If porcupines can look sheepish, the two parents did. Spickle, in yet another corner, just looked bewildered.

'They will be here very soon! Block the entrance!'

One of the meerkats spoke aggressively to the male porcupine. Nungu seemed to hesitate. Another meerkat walked over to where Spickle sat and nipped him on the side of his face, with sharp teeth. Spickle squealed in pain. Nungunungu rattled their quills in anger, then thought better of it. In this confined space they would not be able to manoeuvre their long, unwieldy weapons effectively, and could easily be attacked from in front.

Nungu backed towards the tunnel and raised his spines until they were jammed into the roof and walls. There was now no way into the chamber.

So Shuffle and Pebble could see the front end of what Tuft and the pursuing Duwara, when they arrived outside, could see only the back end of. They could also see what was happening in the chamber; and they were a suffering part of it.

'Stay silent!'

The meerkat who seemed to be leading the Utongo gave Shuffle a quick slash along his flank, as if he did not already have enough wounds. Then he did the same to Pebble, although the poor youngster had not moved where he was huddled. A tiny squeaking from the pups was quickly silenced by three meerkats who lay on top of them, heavily.

Spickle rolled himself into a tight ball, as if he expected to be

105

attacked again.

Shuffle could only guess why the Utongo were behaving in such a way; but he guessed correctly. Duwara were approaching.

'If you move or make a sound we will kill your pups.'

That was to both Pebble and Shuffle.

'If you do not keep the Duwara out we will bite off from your precious little ball of spikes the few quills that he has, and roll him outside for the eagles to eat.'

That was to Nungunungu.

The meerkat did not stop at threats: with his sharp teeth he gripped one of Spickle's quills close to its base, as carefully as if it was a Kisusuli tail, and with a single crunching bite trimmed it off.

Duwara might be approaching; but neither Shuffle nor Pebble could do anything to let them know what was happening in the chamber. They were all under threat of death.

All of that was enough to help Tuft and the others understand what had happened at Rockhome. They were angry at themselves for not stopping long enough to investigate Nungu's strange behaviour. They could have settled that part of the conflict there and then. Now, however, the situation was dire. The rest of Shuffle's story would make that plain.

He was not allowed to tell it yet, however. There was a sudden vibration in the earth around them, and sand pattered down from the roof. Sheena crouched instinctively, fearing that the tunnel was about to collapse on her once more. There was a rush of paws down the tunnel that led most directly from the main entrance, and a young meerkat arrived in a scatter of earth.

'Mbogo!' he cried.

'Mbogo are coming!'

Chapter Twelve: Mbogo

Broad in the head,
Flat in the nose,
Curved in the horn,
Split in the toes.

We snort and stamp,
And you'd better take heed:
That's, oh, more than a bluff –
We also stampede.

Panic spread among the meerkats. Most of them rushed up from the tunnels, leaving Shuffle with Curl and Fara.

Sheena followed, quickly. When she reached the open space in front of the mound, she realised why the meerkats were terrified. Forty or more very large, black animals with enormous thick horns – so curved that they almost curled round on themselves – were moving steadily towards the mound from the direction of the slope, cropping the patchy ground-cover as they came. They looked very heavy. The ground they were feeding on must lie above the chamber with Shuffle in it, and it was their weight that had caused the sand to fall from the roof. If they continued to drift towards the main mound, the tunnels and chambers beneath would collapse. Their arrival could mean the end of much of the Deepden system, in fact. If Nyegere had been a natural disaster, this was more like the end of the world. Something must be done.

Sheena did it. She knew the meerkats themselves would not be capable of halting this ponderous advance, no matter how much jumping and hissing they did. She had only a moment to form a Plan to deal with this Problem. In an instant she selected a target and ran towards it.

She took a grave risk. She had to weave in and out of thick legs like black tree-trunks, and great hooves that were being lifted in no particular order and set down again heavily in the earth. If she had slipped or been knocked off balance by a shifting hoof, she could well have been badly injured.

As she ran among the legs she tried to keep sight of her target. It was the largest of the animals, a great broad-shouldered beast with glaring eyes and a horrible fat, flat, wet nose dribbling slime onto the ground. She had judged it to be the leader of the herd. Two white birds were sitting close together on its head.

She broke out into the space to one side of the animal. Without pausing she jumped up onto its head, causing the birds to flap away in panic. She dug in her claws high up on the animal's bony skull and between its thick, curved horns. Once she was there, it could not see her, no matter how hard it swivelled its dark eyes upwards. All it knew was that its two passengers had suddenly left and another creature, a strange black-and-white one, had flown up from the ground to replace them, and was causing it pain.

Sheena clenched her claws slightly so that they dug a little further in. She was relying on the animal being as slow-witted as it appeared to be. It began to turn in a cumbersome circle, on the spot, as if looking for the thing that was tormenting it. Sheena waited until it was facing back towards the slope and away from

Deepden. Then she called out, 'Up here, bone-brain!'

She freed her claws and gave a little jump down onto the animal's long snout, then beeped its horn – well not its horn exactly, rather its nasty wet nose. She beeped it by reaching forward with a front paw and squeezing it hard, once, twice, making sure her claws went far enough in to cause further pain.

'Beep! Beep!' she said, to add insult to injury. Then she squeezed it once more, much harder, to add injury to insult.

The animal shook its head violently, but she was expecting that and hung on tightly. It then did something else she expected it to do. It set off to chase this out-of-focus black-and-white animal now directly in front of its eyes, trying to run it down and trample it. That was the only way it knew how to deal with things that threatened it. It did not seem to realise that it was carrying the cause of the pain with it as it ran: all it could do was charge forward in blind anger, snorting out clouds of steamy breath as it went – 'Hrrummff! Hrrummff!'

Sheena had guessed correctly. This *was* the herd leader. Where it went, the others followed. She could see them on either side, turning in the same direction and beginning to move. They did so slowly, however, as if reluctant to give up grazing: they did not seem to be aware that anything unusual was happening. Sheena was relieved. She had not wanted to start a thunderous stampede that might have brought about the very thing she was trying to avoid – wholesale collapse of the tunnels beneath.

The great creature continued to lumber heavily in a straight line away from the mounds. Whenever it showed signs of slowing down, she reached forward again with her claws.

'Beep! Beep!'

She even found she could steer it: a little shift of her body to the left, for instance, and a beep on that side of its nose, turned its head slightly in that direction…and its clumsy body followed. She was beginning to enjoy herself.

'Beep! Beep!' went Sheena.

'Hrrummff! Hrrummff' went the animal.

She made sure it kept going until it was well away from Deepden – half-way down the slope, in fact, and off to one side. The other animals had followed steadily, but were now some way behind.

As her strange mount passed under a low branch Sheena released her grip on its bony muzzle and sprang upwards, landing safely on the branch. The animal snorted in surprise, 'Hrrummff!', and stopped suddenly. The black-and-white creature it thought it was chasing had suddenly disappeared. The pain had, too. So it bent its head and began grazing once more, as if it had never moved from the spot where Sheena had hi-jumped it.

'Long horns, short memory!' Sheena said to herself, scornfully.

Almost immediately the two white birds, who must have been flying behind all this while, settled once more on the animal's broad head. Life, for him, was back to normal. All Sheena had to do was wait until he had moved away from the foot of the tree, then jump down and run back towards Deepden – taking care to go round instead of through the herd, who were now, also, grazing again as if nothing had happened.

She could not resist, however, calling out, 'Beep! Beep!' once more, over her shoulder.

She passed quite close to the last animal in the herd, a little way beyond the others. It looked up, briefly, and made the only noise she had heard from any of them, this time rather absent-mindedly:

'Hrrummff!'

All the way through this wild event Sheena had been trying to remember the name of these creatures. Now she thought she knew. Hrrummffaloes.

Chapter Thirteen: Makole

Looked after with care
But not as guests,
Used to make demands,
Not requests.

She got back to Deepden just in time to hear the rest of Shuffle's story.

The meerkats were still outside the burrow when she arrived, reluctant to go back down until they knew the danger was fully over. They had been able to see most of what had happened. They jumped up and down as Sheena approached, but not in any hostile manner: this was an expression of relief, gratitude, and some amazement. They knew how close disaster had come.

'Once more, little cat, once more,' said Tuft, quietly, and Sheena knew what he meant.

The rest of Shuffle's story, in fact, was a message rather than a narrative. He had been given it by the Utongo to carry back to the Duwara. He spoke it faintly, still lying where Sheena had last seen him, with some of the sand from the roof on his fur and in his wounds. He would need to be licked clean soon.

He used the exact Utongo words.

'We have a use for your pups.

'We will give them back to you, however, if you wish. In

return we want the place you call Rockhome. You must destroy the tunnels that lead to it from Deepden, and never come there again.'

That was all. There was no explanation of what use they might have for the Duwara pups, and no mention of Pebble.

Later, back on the surface, the tribe debated the situation. Crossclaw spoke first. For him Rockhome was the most important issue.

'How dare they talk about *the tunnels that lead there from Deepden*! Rockhome *is* Deepden, one of the oldest parts of the burrow. Some of our history is in those caves. Some of our finest

113

forebears made the Rockhome tunnels and chambers, and lived and died there. If we lose Rockhome, we lose a part of our past and a part of ourselves. Deepden will be diminished, Duwara will be diminished.'

Crossclaw's outburst, even though short, exhausted him: by the time he had ended it his old body was shaking.

'We will also lose The Gorge.' Sandstepper was quick to voice his opinion.

'The Utongo will not allow us to pass Rockhome, once they control it. We will starve when the dry times come. And where will we get the special herbs the Ndugu need to do their healing work?'

Sandstepper had recently been made keenly aware of how important the work of the Ndugu was to the tribe.

Sheena had listened to Dad Allen often enough to have some understanding of the kind of arguments being used. If Thomas and Amy's father had been there now he would have said something very teacherish like, 'Ah, the economic justification here is stronger than the historical one.'

Sheena would have agreed with him, teacherish though his comments might have been. Being a cat, she had little interest in events that had already taken place: once they were over, they were over. Cats live very completely in the present, and have an eye half-open to the future only to ensure that today's good things will be here tomorrow. She had no tribal memory either, since she had never lived in a tribe (or whatever a collection of cats might be called). So she saw little point in making a fuss about Rockhome just because of what it once was. Now it was only a hole among some big stones, more trouble than it was worth. The Utongo had got in through there, hadn't they?

'It's time history became history,' she thought to herself.

114

It always seemed to be the male of the species who got himself all in a twist about such things. 'Maybe we should have herstory instead.'

Although Moon, when she spoke, did not express that thought exactly, she seemed to see things in the same way.

'Never mind Rockhome,' she said. 'We can always dig another Rockhome if we need one. Why do you males always want to fight over places? It's much more important to get the pups back.'

Crossclaw was quick to reply. 'You say we can always dig another Rockhome. There can never be another Rockhome. There can be more pups.'

'But there can be no more pups exactly the same as *those* pups,' Moon said. 'Every pup is once for all. If we lose this litter to the Utongo we have lost something special, and lost it forever.'

'And the pups will *become* Utongo,' Tuft added. 'They are pure Duwara: we cannot allow them to be brought up under the Other Sun. That would be a betrayal of the One *True* Sun.'

'Aha! The religious argument!' Sheena could imagine Dad Allen saying. 'I wondered when that would come up!'

Crossclaw remained silent. Belief in the supremacy of their own sun was another thing that made the Duwara the Duwara: so he was torn.

Stab now spoke up, however.

'The Utongo want to destroy us. This is their way of doing it. If they have Rockhome, they will be able to attack the rest of Deepden whenever they wish. It will be too easy for them to open up the tunnels and sneak in on us while we sleep.'

'We must not give it up so easily.'

Stab's argument was the military one. Did the Utongo really want the whole of Deepden to themselves, however? Sheena wondered how the Duwara had learned that.

'We need to know why they want the pups,' said Tuft, 'if not just as hostages to make us do things we do not want to do. Then we might be able to find another way of getting them back. We need a dunzi in Longburrow.'

That was why Sheena went through The Gorge.

Chapter Fourteen: Kinyonga

A camel with an h but no hump,
A lion with a mane but no teeth;
In a tree we match its leaves,
On the ground, the earth beneath.

It was dark among the trees. There were large bushes between the tree-trunks, growing closely together; and above them was a canopy of leaves. Together, trees and bushes kept the sunlight out completely, and the world of The Gorge was a sombre green.

Tuft had advised her to head across the plain towards Rockhome, then strike out directly towards The Gorge just past the Rockhome mound. Other routes down into the steep valley, and up its further side, might prove too difficult for her, although meerkats could manage them well enough.

She took a few steps into the gloom; then she went back out for one last look at the sun. She wanted to remember exactly what it looked like on this side of The Gorge. She stared at it too long, however, and its image burnt itself onto the back of her eyes (it might have helped to have a pair of meerkat sunglasses) so that after she had turned and re-entered the woodland it was some time before she could see properly again.

She did not know how long it would take her to get through The Gorge, nor what reception she might get from the Utongo when she arrived at Longburrow – if she even managed to travel so far without being challenged and turned back…or worse.

Before any of that happened she had to think up an account of what she was doing there (*there* being wherever it would be that she next encountered the Utongo). She would no doubt have been seen by them, earlier, in company with the Duwara. How could she explain *that*?

As she worked her way carefully through the bushes, Sheena thought some more about the two suns question. She had examined The Gorge carefully as she walked towards it, and could now begin to understand how the two meerkat tribes had become rivals, then enemies, and why each believed it had its own sun.

The Gorge was very long. It stretched sideways across Sheena's path from one horizon to the other. It was more than likely that no meerkat had ever travelled around it at either end. So a belief had grown up that it separated two worlds, the Utongo and the Duwara. There was a sun, a different sun, in each world. That was why the two tribes were different…or so the meerkats thought.

Soon after she began moving further into the greenery she had to change direction slightly. She detected a rustling in the undergrowth some way off to one side. She did the sensible thing and just stopped, hidden behind some large leaves trailing on the ground. A group of meerkats passed from right to left not very far in front of where she was, and disappeared ahead of her and to the left. It looked as if they were on patrol: they were moving slowly and looking round carefully. Twice while Sheena was watching them they halted and did much sniffing on the ground. One or two of them backed up towards other low-hanging branches and sprayed their scent on the leaves.

'Utongo,' Sheena decided.

'They really are taking over here.'

She waited for some time after they had disappeared; then she moved forward again, but at an angle away from the line they had taken.

The ground began to fall away in front of her. It became rockier, then steeper. Soon she was having to jump down from one level to another. After a short while it flattened out, before dropping away again. The Gorge was much deeper than she had expected, and the further down she went the gloomier it became.

She reached another level stretch. As she went forward across it an eye caught her eye. It belonged to a large leaf on a bush up ahead. It was set into the top of a little, wrinkled green mound near the leaf's pointed end. It swivelled jerkily, up, down, around, pausing briefly between each movement.

Sheena began to move cautiously past the bush. The eye swung round to watch her, then looked away again. Then another eye appeared, on a different part of the leaf. It too swivelled towards her, then away, and the first eye came back to scrutinise her once more. The leaf was keeping an eye on her, one eye at a time.

'But leaves don't have eyes!' Sheena thought.

Then as she stared at the pattern made by the foliage, a shape began to stand out, as if from one of the Magic Eye designs Thomas spent a lot of time dizzying himself with. A short fat lizard with a curved back was clinging to the branch with what looked like split feet. His lumpy head had a fringe on top and an eye sticking a long way out on either side; and the eyes, Sheena could now see, moved independently of one another.

'Hello! That's a good trick! Can you see two different things at the same time? That must be confusing, unless you've got two brains.'

Sheena had decided to be friendly. This lizard was not much more than half her size, and didn't look at all dangerous; in fact the way his eyes were moving made him look rather shifty.

'Hello, by the way. I'm Sheena. I'm a cat.'

'I'm Kinyonga. I'm whatever I want to be.'

What on earth did that mean? Perhaps it was something to do with having independent eyes and two brains.

Would having two brains make it easier to believe there were two suns? Maybe a little bit of research would be in order: anything that might help in her dealings with the Utongo would be welcome. What did other creatures round here believe about the sun?

'Pardon me for asking, but can you tell me how many suns there are?'

'What's a sun?'

The lizard's voice was muffled, as if he had a mouthful of something.

That was as far as Sheena's research got. She had started from a wrong premise. She had not realised until now that there might be creatures on the earth who had never seen one sun, let alone two.

'The sun's what we see by.'

That was the simplest answer Sheena could give.

'I don't have a sun; and I see well enough,' said Kinyonga.

He proved his point. Just then a small insect with transparent wings settled further along the branch, in front of the lizard but twice as far away from it as the lizard was long. Kinyonga's eyes swivelled forward so that for once they were both looking at the same thing at the same time. He rocked back and forward, slowly, several times.

There was a pause, then, 'Whap!'

Kinyonga

Almost too fast for Sheena to see, Kinyonga's very, very long tongue had whipped out and struck the insect, then disappeared back inside his mouth. The insect was no longer on the branch. That perhaps explained why the lizard's voice had been muffled: his mouth was full of tongue. Now it was full of insect as well, and one twitching leg was sticking out from between Kinyonga's thin lips.

How had he actually caught the insect, however?

'How did you do that?' Sheena asked. She wondered whether she could train her own tongue to perform a similar trick. She had been very envious of a monitor lizard she once met, who could smell with his. Perhaps she could use her tongue to reach out for her little cat biscuits, to save her the trouble of getting up and walking over to her dish. Her milk might be more of a problem, however.

Kinyonga had been chewing slowly. Now he gulped and the insect's legs disappeared.

'I did *that* like *this*,' he said.

He rocked back and forward again for a short while, holding tight to the branch. Sheena decided that this was to help him judge the exact distance to his target. Then he shot his tongue out again, 'Whap!' – but this time he had aimed only for a leaf. His tongue hit the leaf and stuck to it, so that when he drew it back again the leaf, and the thin twig it was attached to, were pulled a little way towards him. Then he let go of the leaf, which sprang back into place, and his tongue disappeared into his mouth once more.

Sheena had sometimes watched Dad Allen working on *Great White*'s engine. He spent lots of time doing that, even though it didn't seem he was very good at it – he also had to spend lots of money paying local mechanics to put right the things he had done wrong.

On one particular occasion he had dropped a bolt into a narrow gap down the side of the engine, and couldn't reach in far enough with his fingers to get it out. He was soon at the muttering stage.

'Here Dad, try this!'

Thomas, who was also watching, had learned a trick from somewhere. He picked up a long, straight twig from the ground nearby and stuck a lump of chewing gum on the end. On this occasion Dad Allen chose to ignore the fact that Thomas had chewing gum: he took the twig, poked it down into the gap and lifted it out with the bolt embedded in the sticky lump at the end. (He dropped the bolt in again soon after, and couldn't get it back this time; but Mum Allen told him he shouldn't worry because Land Rovers were designed to carry on working even after all their nuts and bolts had shaken loose and fallen out.)

Perhaps there was a lump of something like chewing gum (spearmint?) on the end of this weapon Kinyonga had instead of a normal tongue.

Sheena could now see why at first she had failed to spot the whole lizard. His lumpy skin was a dark mottled green, and matched perfectly the leaves surrounding him. That meant he would not be noticed by insects settling nearby, until it was too late. 'Whap!' would be the first thing they knew of the situation, and 'Crunch!' would be the last.

'Let me show you something else,' said Kinyonga.

He moved backwards along the branch, slowly, stepped delicately down onto another branch and from there down to the ground. Once on the bare earth, he stopped. For a moment he was easy to see, green against patchy brown. As Sheena watched, however, his greenness changed to a murky grey and then to an uneven brown perfectly matching the colour of the soil on which he stood. An insect settling *here* would not see the lizard either, and it would simply be a matter once more of 'Whap! Crunch! Thanks for lunch!'

'We don't do that just to catch things,' said Kinyonga. 'We also do it to hide from birds and snakes.

'More often we do it just to show what mood we're in.'

People changed colour according to their mood, Sheena knew (Dad Allen's face had gone red with annoyance, for instance, when he was trying to get his fingers round the dropped bolt the first time; then it went pink with embarrassment when he dropped it a second time) but she hadn't realised other creatures did it as well.

'Sometimes it's just because the temperature around us has changed,' said Kinyonga.

'But *how* do you do it?'

Sheena had decided she'd quite like to learn this camouflage trick as well – it would be even more useful than knowing how to shoot her tongue out, especially whenever she was in Baragandiri. Her black and white fur was a real disadvantage here.

'We do it by believing it. When I want to look like a leaf, I decide I'm a leaf; when I'm on the ground, I *am* the ground. It's all a matter of faith. Our species has lots of that.'

Sheena couldn't think what species he was a member of. She knew a bit about belief and faith, however, and what they could do to you and for you. Her old friend Mpole the gradual elephant had believed he was slow in the brain, and that had slowed his brain right down; then he had developed some faith in himself and become an elephant to be reckoned with. It seemed you could persuade yourself to be (or not be) anything you wanted. But to be a leaf? Surely that was a bit extreme.

Maybe she could learn something from this creature, however. She was soon going to need to put on a disguise of her own, and she would have to have faith in it.

Now it was time to continue her journey through The Gorge.

'Thank you for those most interesting demonstrations,' she said. Then she searched for a polite way of saying goodbye.

'May your tongue always be long and sticky.'

Perhaps Kinyonga thought she was being sarcastic, perhaps he was just in a playful mood (what was the colour for that?)…but whatever the reason, as Sheena turned her back to walk away he unleashed his tongue at her, just like Thomas sometimes flicked his towel at Amy when they had been swimming.

'Whap!' it went on Sheena's rump, and she jumped and ran. The end of Kinyonga's tongue had failed to stick to her fur, and he would be left with a mouthful of cat hairs.

'Serves him right!' Sheena thought.

As she ran she wondered which eye was watching her leave.

Chapter Fifteen: Mondo

Little more than slave,
But not quite servile.
The squeak of a mouse
Makes me smile.

Between big and small,
And feline by definition,
Change reveals my name
Without repetition.

The further she went down into The Gorge, the more the darkness under the trees deepened. In some ways this was an even more worrying place to be than the Deepden tunnels. Because the vegetation was so dense Sheena could not see much further ahead than she had been able to do underground; and the general silence there had been replaced by a continuous rustling here, and once by a low growl, another time by a violent fluttering in the trees overhead. The fact that this was meerkat territory, and now Utongo territory, did not mean there were not lots of other creatures around; but she saw nothing moving.

Eventually she was within sight of what must be The Gorge's lowest point, although she was still quite high above it, on a final flat stretch in the overall downwards drop. There were signs of water down there, but no water. Smoothly curved piles of sand, almost small beaches, had been created at some point by a swiftly running stream. Piles of debris – broken branches and old leaves – now lay along the dry stream bed. The roots of some of the trees were exposed where the earth had been washed away.

Just as Sheena was preparing for the last part of the descent, she realised she was being watched. She was about to have some help with her disguise – but at a price.

The animal that would change her appearance was not well hidden. Its coat was pale gold with black spots, and it stood out clearly against the rock face at the end of the wide ledge on which Sheena now hesitated.

It was a female cat…but what a cat! She was not one of what were called the Big Cats – lions, leopards, cheetahs – but she was not a small cat (like Sheena) either. She had remarkably long legs, her back ones even longer than her front ones so that her whole body was tipped slightly forwards as if she was leaning into a run. Her head was very small for her body, and her ears were very big for her head. She looked as if she had been stretched, and Sheena was reminded of those slinky, long-limbed fashion models on tv that Dad Allen pretended not to watch.

'Welcome,' said this splendid cat. She extended each leg in turn, languorously, as if she were trying to rid them of a stiffness; but Sheena also had the feeling that they were being held out for her to admire. Each set of claws at the end of a leg looked polished and sharpened, and there was a light perfumy smell in the air. This feminine creature obviously looked after herself very well.

'I'm Mondo.'

She paused, as if she expected Sheena to know what that meant.

'You're just in time.'

'In time for what?'

'In time to stop me getting bored. There's not much happening down here today.'

'Sorry, can't stop for a chat, not even a cat-chat,' said Sheena. 'I'm on my way to visit some enemies.'

She hadn't meant to say that, but there was something about this tall, confident animal that unnerved her.

'I wasn't thinking of a chat. I had in mind more of a challenge.'

So this strange cat's stretching had been in preparation for some kind of sporting competition – jumping, perhaps? Surely not running, in this steep, rugged place.

'Sorry, can't stop for a challenge.'

Sheena was facing enough of a challenge already.

'You've already got one. It's to get past me,' Mondo said.

That didn't look too difficult. Mondo was some way off. A single leap would take Sheena down to the next level, away from this cool, stylish creature. She took a step forward.

There was a sudden light thud and a flurry of earth. Mondo had landed in front of her and was barring her way. She must have sprung superbly from her standing position near the rock face, using her long legs. She was considerably taller than Sheena, and looked down at her through narrowed eyes. Her small head made her seem mean. Her long legs and large claws made her seem dangerous. She spoke casually, however.

'First point to you, for one step forward.

'Next point to me.'

As she said that, she became very un-casual. She lashed out at Sheena with a front paw, and caught her on the cheek, just below her eye. The pain was sharp, and Sheena felt blood trickling down through her fur.

'One point for a step forward. One point for a blow landed. So that's one-all.'

Mondo took a quick step forward herself, and Sheena instinctively moved backwards.

'Two-one to me. First to ten points wins. If it's you, you can leave. If it's me, you can leave the way you came – if you can walk, that is.'

The strange cat stepped forward again.

'Three-one to me.'

This situation was moving on much too quickly.

Sheena was not a fighting cat. When she could not avoid a confrontation she preferred to win it by bluff or cheek. It seemed there was no choice here, however. She flicked her paw out towards Mondo's face.

She missed. The other cat had swiftly jerked her head back on the end of her long neck. Then she struck with her own paw again, and her claws tore deeply into Sheena's shoulder.

'Four-one.'

Sheena's opponent had the advantage of a much longer reach.

'Five-one.'

She had gashed Sheena's neck, almost before Sheena saw the blow coming.

Sheena would have to try some in-fighting. She took a sudden step forwards, close in to Mondo, who lashed out again – but this time her paw passed over Sheena's shoulder and failed to make contact.

'Five-two,' said Sheena, and she stepped forward once more so that she was tight up against her adversary. With her shorter front legs she was able to reach up and get in two quick slashes to Mondo's chest.

'Five-all,' she said.

Mondo did not like that at all: she hissed sharply; but she had a strategy of her own. She suddenly sprang up and over Sheena's head, twisting in the air as she did so and ripping one of Sheena's ears.

'One more for a blow landed, double points for a forwards leap. Eight-five.'

It seemed the rules of this game could be modified as Mondo saw fit.

Sheena was capable of a little rule play of her own, however. She was still facing towards the bottom of The Gorge. That for her was forward, technically speaking: she chose to ignore the fact that her opponent was now behind her. She took two quick steps towards the end of the level patch of ground, tucked her herself into a ball just like Spickle had done, and rolled off the edge.

'Two points for each step forward, and triple points for a forward roll! I win!' she called out; but her voice was probably too muffled to be heard.

She had no choice about where or how fast she would roll. It was very fast downwards, and a long way downwards.

Her body was not protected by spines, but her fur was quite thick, and springy. She gathered speed as she went, at times leaving the ground altogether. She felt herself bump into two boulders on her way down, but only the second blow was severe, and neither caused her speed to slacken.

At the bottom of the slope she crashed into a pile of thorny branches. That stopped her without causing major injury, but the thorns raked along her sides, and scratched her some more as she struggled out of the pile.

It was a very different-looking cat who began the long, painful climb up the far side of The Gorge.

Chapter Sixteen: Papasi

I have eight legs but crawl up one.
I burrow but not in the ground.
The name of my food also ends in —ood.
I start off flat and end up round.

The climb upwards was very difficult indeed. The bushes were low and thorny and she had to work her way round some rock faces too high to jump up.

She was bleeding from many wounds. She had been slashed several times. Her shoulder had been badly hurt when she collided with the second boulder: a lump of fur and skin had been torn off, leaving a pink, weeping patch of flesh, and the joint was stiffening rapidly. Her poor stump of a tail had dragged along the ground at some point, and the end was raw and red.

She was relieved when the climb became less steep and the light grew stronger. The bushes gradually thinned out. She must be close to the far side of The Gorge. That meant, however, that she was also closer to Longburrow. She needed to get her story ready.

Mondo had not pursued her as she rolled and bounced down the slope. Perhaps the other, larger cat was licking her own wounds, and her scratched pride. What kind of other cat had she been? A serval cat perhaps? Wasn't that what Spickle had thought Sheena was? A cat to stay clear of, in any case, Sheena decided.

131

By damaging her so badly, however, Mondo had done her a favour, as things turned out.

She reached the edge of the strip of woodland. She was not sorry to see the bright sunlight through the last of the trees, whichever sun it was coming from.

At some distance across the plain on this side of The Gorge, she could see many sandy mounds. Did they mark the entrances to Longburrow? They seem to be in a long, zig-zagging line, running roughly parallel to the Gorge itself and the stretch of smaller trees among which Sheena was now standing.

She suddenly felt weak, and sank back on her haunches, still in the shade. She rested like that for some time, licking those of her wounds she could reach.

She realised she had another problem in addition to her injuries. As she carefully cleaned herself, her tongue found hard little lumps attached to the skin in various parts of her body. She knew what they were. They were ticks – tough-shelled insects that drilled into animals' flesh and slowly drained their blood.

Like most cats Sheena had suffered from fleas every now and again, but she knew how to deal with them. The thought of these larger parasites, like beetles with saw-toothed mouth-parts, fastening themselves onto her and cutting their way through her skin to suck her blood – that was much worse. They must have clung to her legs as she brushed through the undergrowth in The Gorge, and crawled up to her body, then secretly bored their way into her when they found a place they liked.

She made only a half-hearted attempt to nip with her teeth the few ticks she could reach: they were hard, and shiny, and slippery. She could not simply pull them off, either. They would have come apart at the neck and their horrible heads with their jagged mouths would have remained locked in place and caused her

132

flesh to fester. There was no way to rid herself of them: she would just have to try not to think about them for the time being.

She was reluctant to step out into the open. For one thing she was not sure that she would be able to complete her journey across the hot bare ground in her weakened state: just to look out into the glare made her feel light-headed. For another she had not yet worked out what to say when she was challenged by the Utongo.

The Utongo themselves solved both problems for her.

Just in front of the trees a low embankment dropped away onto the open plain. Sheena had barely noticed it. Several meerkat heads suddenly popped up along its line, then the whole meerkat group bounded forward into the trees and encircled her. They were a fierce-looking bunch, standing confidently on their hind legs with their pointed faces directed questioningly towards her and their curved lower canines showing. Even if she had not been feeling so torn and battered, Sheena would have been intimidated by them.

It turned out that there was a tunnel entrance in the face of the embankment, out of sight from where Sheena had come to a halt. She had been seen by a look-out on the nearest mound out on the plain, and this party of meerkats had scurried along underground to what was one of the Longburrow outposts, much closer to The Gorge than Sheena had expected it to be and much nearer than any of the Duwara tunnels on the other side. The Utongo take-over of The Gorge had been long in the planning.

Not only did they know she was there, they knew who she was; and they made a large, wrong assumption about *why* she was there.

'So, they've driven you out, have they? Very good at that,

those ungrateful Duwara. I suppose it's because you weren't any use to them after all, when it came to a fight.

'They made you pay first, though, didn't they? They did a good job there, at least.'

Sheena could only imagine what she looked like. She knew she was bleeding again, in several places – cleaning the gashes in her flesh had opened them up once more. Her ear was badly torn. Fur was missing from her shoulder. She had lost two claws.

So she was in disguise after all, thanks to Mondo – as a victim of the Duwara.

'They've even bitten your tail off. Did they think it was poisonous?'

Just the thought of having her tail bitten off made her feel faint, after what she had just been through. She remembered only too well how she had really lost it and how painful that had been…and as she was remembering she felt herself fall sideways

into unconsciousness and land on the ground with a strangely distant thud.

She had passed out in the shade of a tree. When she woke again the sun had dropped a little in the sky, and was now shining directly on her where she lay. She felt very hot and very unwell. Most of the meerkats had disappeared, leaving only two. The larger group had obviously decided that in her present state she was no threat. The remaining pair showed none of the earlier fierceness that had frightened Sheena.

'Here, these are for you,' said one. Two white grubs were wriggling on the ground, and he pushed them towards her. (The meerkat answer to most problems was to eat a little something.)

Sheena was suspicious. These were Utongo, after all. She was very thirsty, however. She rolled over painfully onto her stomach, sniffed the grubs, decided they were safe, then picked them up one by one with her teeth and ate them. They were hardly a meal, but their juiciness was welcome in her badly parched mouth.

'You need to come with us,' said the larger of the two meerkats.

'The sun will go down before too long, and this is no place at night for an injured animal.'

Why were they being so friendly towards her? Because they thought the Duwara had been cruel? That didn't seem like the Utongo. From what she had seen and heard of them they themselves were anything but kind.

'You're probably wondering why we want to help you. There's an old Utongo saying, *The foe of my foe is my friend.* We assume you're now a foe of the Duwara...so Welcome, Friend.

'We will ask something in return for our welcome, however. We will want to know what you know about the Duwara and their plans. It is a long time since any of us had any business with them other than the business of battle.

'You must come with us into Longburrow. We will enter here, at The Gorge Tunnel, and travel underground to Heartmound. That will keep you out of the sun.'

Sheena looked up at the sun for the first time since she had emerged from the darkness of The Gorge. It hurt her eyes, and she had to look away before she was able to compare it with what she remembered of the sun she had left behind.

'Which sun is it?' she asked.

She was beginning to remember why she was here. She was supposed to be a spy. So she ought to start asking spy-type questions. More than that, however, she was beginning to have doubts herself over the question of suns. She could not be sure, now, after all that had happened to her in the darkness of the trees, that this was the same sun she had seen from the Deepden side of The Gorge.

'The Utongo sun, of course – the True Sun.'

She had soon left the sun, True or Not True, behind, and was travelling painfully but steadily down into the darkness of The Gorge Tunnel. She had no idea what she would find at the end of it.

Chapter Seventeen: Fadhila

Rhymes with blindness
But can open your eyes.
Beware, however:
It may be just a disguise.

One underground chamber was much like another, Sheena decided; the only difference, sometimes, was size. The one she was now lying in seemed identical to the one in Deepden she had occupied with Pebble and Sandstepper. Even the smell seemed the same – Utongo meerkats probably peed on each other while they slept, just like Duwara. No doubt a meerkat would be able to tell the tribal smells apart, but Sheena could not.

The two males who had stayed with her at the edge of The Gorge and had helped her down into Longburrow had remained with her here also. They were just outside the chamber now, in what was a very wide tunnel. Were they guarding her? It didn't much matter: she had no intention of moving far, nor indeed of moving at all. She had a deal of recovering to do.

She had suffered much in The Gorge, and she knew she had been lucky to get all the way through it. It was a deep and mysterious place, and she could have been met by creatures more terrible, and forces more powerful, than Mondo, deceitful and vicious though the serval cat had proved. She would hesitate before entering it again, even if in the end she had to do so in order to get back to Deepden, and then to the campsite.

She had talked to the two meerkats, a little. The larger one was Tassel, the smaller Streak.

'*Why Tassel?* Look at my tail.'

Sheena didn't need to: she had already noticed it as she walked unsteadily behind him on the long underground journey from The Gorge. It ended in a droopy brush of hair, which sometimes dragged on the ground.

'*Why Streak?* Look at my back.'

There was a long strip of whiteish hair running down Streak's spine, at right angles to the darker lateral bars.

Sheena had also been tended to by two female Utongo. It seemed the Utongo, like the Duwara, had Ndugu – Sisters, who knew about healing. They had brought her more food, had licked the wounds she could not reach, and had cracked her ticks one by one with their clever little teeth, so that a little of the blood they

had already drawn from her leaked out into her fur. The ticks would now die, and drop off. Sheena had listened for the sound of the Ndugu licking their lips after each crunch, but had not heard it…which she found reassuring.

She had insisted on dealing herself, however, with the raw and sensitive end of her tail.

All of this was very different from what she had expected. Either these meerkats were just pretending to be friendly, or there was another group of Utongo somewhere in Longburrow who were capable of the cruel things that had happened in Deepden. If the latter, she would need to be very careful when she met them.

That would not be until the next day. It was obviously sleep time for the meerkats. All four of them, Tassel, Streak and the two Ndugu, curled up together in a heap outside the chamber entrance, and immediately became still. Sheena suddenly felt alone, as if they'd gone somewhere without her. There was silence in the tunnels.

Chapter Eighteen: Dunzi

I do it with my little eye
As sly as any sleuth;
But I also work by means of words
To find the hidden truth.

She rested through the night, sometimes awake, sometimes dozing, but always aware of the slight sounds that could be heard now and again – a sigh from the one of the meerkats, a small scratching somewhere in the earth near her head, a trickle of sand in one corner of the chamber.

She was awake when the meerkats stirred. She felt chilled: overnight the temperature underground seemed to have dropped considerably, and she had not had a pile of meerkats to burrow into.

Tassel and Streak stood on their hind legs, stretched, yawned, staggered a little, dropped forward onto all fours and left for the surface. The two Ndugu set about cleaning Sheena's wounds once more.

'The sun will rise soon,' said Fade, one of the Ndugu. 'We think you should come with us to the main mound, for Sunwatch. Can you walk so far?

Sheena had walked *very* far, the night before, for one so injured – all the way from The Gorge; so she thought she could manage what was probably only a short distance to the open air.

She was nearly wrong – not about the distance, but about her own strength. Once on her feet and in the tunnel she felt weak again. Her shoulder was very stiff and painful, so she slowed right down; but she still became dizzy after only a few minutes' climb up the sloping passageway.

By the time they reached the outside, the sun was just about to show above the flat horizon.

There were several Utongo on top of the mound she and the Ndugu emerged from, and in the half-light she could see numbers of other meerkats on the mounds nearby. They were all in standard meerkat posture, upright and with their front paws hanging down in front of them. They were very still.

Then the top edge of the sun showed above the dark landscape, and the sharpness of its rays made Sheena blink. She had decided not to climb up onto the mound: it would have hurt too much; and it was the same sun to be seen from down here (wasn't it?)

It seemed important to the meerkats, however, that they be close together when the sun rose, as if that was necessary for it to fully do its work; so Fade and her companion jumped up alongside Tassel and Streak, who were already there (but looking sleepy still).

The tunnel they had used to get here came out at the back of the mound, and from where Sheena now stood the meerkats above her were silhouetted against the brightening sky. As the sun climbed into full view, the outline of their fur began to glow so that the dark shapes of their bodies were richly edged in gold.

When the sun's first warmth reached them, the same remarkable change came over the Utongo of Longburrow as Sheena had seen in the Duwara of Deepden. Sunwatch was the Utongo equivalent of Sunwake. There was a straightening of bodies, and a brightening of eyes, and a sharpening of look; and the meerkats stood motionless for a long while in their straightened and brightened and sharpened state.

Sheena herself felt the warmth, and something of the same renewal (as she had on Deepden Mound), but also some of the apartness she had experienced the previous night down in the chamber, when the meerkats had fallen asleep together in their warm pile.

She was not a meerkat; and perhaps she was a mere cat after all, a solitary creature without the comforts and strengths of a shared life, and without some of its meaning. Who would have cared if she had died in the depths of The Gorge as a result of Mondo's nasty attack? Only a human boy and girl, perhaps, too far from here in any case to know what had happened to her.

It seemed that this early morning sun had the power not only to warm, and to heal (her wounds hurt less than they had done in the cold chamber), and to bring together, but also to stir thoughts about more deeply personal things.

Sheena's own thoughts were interrupted by a young meerkat on whom Sunwatch had not yet had the desired effect: he dozed off, lost his footing and slithered down the back of the mound, feet-first and face-down, landing with a squeak. Young Utongo meerkats had some of the same problems as Young Duwara, it seemed.

Sheena looked along the length of Longburrow. Even from ground level she could see that the system had a layout different from that of Deepden. The Longburrow mounds stretched over a great distance, in a roughly straight line. The Deepden mounds, in contrast, had been set out in something like a (very large) circle, with only Rockhome well outside the perimeter.

The sun was now well clear of the horizon. The meerkats on all the mounds, near and far, continued in their upright position.

Sunwatch had gone on much longer than Sunwake, Sheena decided.

At that moment, however, a commotion began at the mound furthest away in one direction. The meerkats there had leapt down and were setting off on their first breakfast forage, making a lot of noise as they did so. Sheena could hear their chirrups and squeaks even from that distance.

None of the meerkats on the other mounds moved, however.

Three meerkats from that furthest mound headed straight for the next in line. When they reached it there was a pause, then the jumping down, squeaking and chirruping broke out there also, as if those meerkats had just been freed to begin the next part of

the daily ceremony. The trio carried on to the next mound and the next after that, coming closer all the time. Their arrival at each mound had the same effect – an explosion of cheerful meerkats.

As the three meerkats came near, Sheena noted that the one in the middle was larger than any meerkat she had so far seen.

Tassel spoke down to her, quietly, from where he stood above her on the mound.

'Do not move when Slash arrives. He will want to speak to you.'

The meerkats stopped when they reached Heartmound. The large one stepped forward. Sheena did not have to try very hard to work out how he had got his name. Not only were his claws long and cruel-looking, both his voice and his eyes were sharp and angry. Either he was a bad-tempered meerkat by nature or he was badly in need of breakfast.

He did not speak to Sheena after all. Instead he looked at her, long and hard and piercingly. She felt as if the word 'Dunzi' was written across her forehead, and for a brief moment her paws moved nervously in the sand.

Then Slash turned away from her, and did not look in her direction again. He addressed the whole group on the mound; but he seemed throughout to be looking principally at Tassel and Streak.

'So this is the animal I have been told about? The one who was with the Duwara? Why do you think she will be useful to us? Has she told you anything?

'Why is she out here, anyway, where she could run away? She should have been kept in the chambers until I questioned her. Take her back down now! Make sure she is guarded well!'

The questions and the orders had come thick and fast and harshly. Sheena felt herself bristle (a bit like a porcupine). She bit back a rude comment. She must remember she was a dunzi, and say as little as possible but see as much as she could.

Perhaps there was more to be discovered in the depths of Longburrow. So she allowed herself to be led back down into the tunnel by Tassel and Streak. She hoped they would not be punished for their friendliness towards her.

As she was about to enter the tunnel she saw that Slash and his two companions had set off for the next mound along the line, where the meerkats were still standing to what now seemed to Sheena more like attention. The whole process, in fact, appeared to be some sort of military inspection. The Utongo were really taking this war seriously.

Soon she was back in the chamber, not altogether unhappy at being able to lie down in the coolness once more and rest her aching body. She hoped Fade would be allowed to come to her. If she was to get her strength back she would have to have food as well as rest; and her wounds would need more cleaning if they were to heal

Streak had left, but Tassel had stayed to talk.

'So now you have seen the whole of Longburrow, at least from the outside. It is an excellent place. It has been our home forever.'

'It's very big,' said Sheena. 'Is it still growing?'

That seemed like a good spying sort of question.

'We don't need it to be any bigger. There is more than enough room for all of us. And we don't think the tribe will get any larger. In fact it may get smaller, if more of us die.'

'Were some of you killed when you fought the Duwara, then?'

'Some, yes. Others died straight afterwards. More may still die. But that is not what I meant.'

'Then are you just talking about Utongo meerkats dying

145

because they're *old?*'

'No. Enough pups are usually born to make up for those who die naturally, or are killed by other animals.

'But now we have a sickness among us. A young meerkat came to us from Deepden several months ago. He asked to join our tribe. That was when such things were still allowed.

'We think he was sent deliberately. He was sick, and died. We believe he was sick before he left Deepden. Soon after he arrived, some of our younger meerkats started to fall ill, and several of them died also. We think the Duwara wanted him to bring his disease to us so that we would be wiped out. That's the kind of meerkats the Duwara are. That is what their sun has turned them into. What they cannot get by fighting they try to take by other means.

'We think they want Longburrow for themselves. We know they want The Gorge. That is why we have taken it now, to stop their advance.'

This was all very strange, Sheena thought. She had heard nothing from Sandstepper or Tuft or Stab about wanting to take over Longburrow, or even The Gorge, and certainly nothing about sending diseased meerkats among the Utongo to kill them off.

'Now our pups die too, of the same sickness. We have lost too many.'

'Is that why you have taken Duwara pups?'

'Yes – to replace some of ours; and to strengthen our blood; and to punish the Duwara; and to make sure they do not grow to outnumber us. We will take more of their pups as time goes on. It was not too hard the first time, and we have learnt how to deal with Nungunungu.

'It will be even easier when Rockhome becomes ours.'

146

With a shock Sheena realised Tassel had been part of the Utongo raiding party. This mild-mannered, helpful meerkat had been one of those who had behaved so cruelly at Rockhome.

'How do you know that the pups you have taken do not have the disease also? And what about that other meerkat who disappeared? What was his name? Stone? Did you bring him here too? Perhaps he's sick, too. He looked sick, the last time I saw him.'

Sometimes, as a spy, it was a good idea to pretend to know less than you did. Sheena had learned that among the lions of Baragandiri.

'We have put them all, the Duwara pups and him, in a separate part of Longburrow until we are sure they are not carrying the disease.'

'And then?'

Sheena did want to hear about Pebble, where he was, and how he was, and what was going to happen to him; but she knew she would have to take care not to ask too many questions too quickly.

'We shall bring up the litter as Utongo – the young meerkat you call Stone also, if he is capable of ridding himself of the influence of the Duwara sun.

'If not, we shall kill him.'

Sheena was startled by the coldness with which Tassel spoke those words. Then he left, abruptly.

Chapter Nineteen: Kenge Tena

Has scales and hisses
But is not a snake.
When he's around
You should stay awake.

Met once before
In a different place;
But of his friendliness then
There's now no trace.

She cat-napped on and off through most of the day. Tassel had been replaced by three new guards. They said nothing to her and did not reply to any of her questions when, towards the end of the day, she tried to start a conversation. Then they just went to sleep. It seemed that meerkats had extreme difficulty doing anything else when night fell.

'Some guards!' Sheena said.

Perhaps they thought cats behaved in the same way. Not this cat: she had other plans (but hardly a Plan, yet). She felt much better than she had done earlier. Fade had visited her twice to bring her small amounts of food. She was no longer bleeding, and her tail had stopped throbbing. She would just have to take great care not to move too quickly and open up her wounds once more.

Her intention was to leave the chamber and explore. She thought it very unlikely that she would be able to find Pebble and the pups, at least at a first attempt. Longburrow stretched a long way in both directions, and only a lucky guess would take her in the right one.

Her guards, however, had lain down, entwined in a pile that blocked the chamber entrance and was too high for her to step over. There was no room to step round. She would have to step through them.

As she set about doing so, she felt as if she was trying to get past a security system like the ones in Thomas's video games, where intruders had to bend, twist and jump their way very carefully though a network of criss-crossing red laser beams. She had always thought she would be good at that. Now was her chance to find out: one wrong move and the alarm would go off.

She picked a spot between two entangled front legs and put a front paw down; then she had to bend sideways to avoid a leg sticking up in the air, and put her other front paw down very carefully between an ear and a tail; then she lifted a rear leg over a head stretched out on the ground.

When she was half-way through the pile of fur-covered limbs, torsos and heads, one of the meerkats suddenly sighed, rolled over, and put a front leg round one of Sheena's, hugging it lovingly. She was forced to stand perfectly still until he sighed once more and rolled over in the opposite direction, freeing her. Then it was bend, lift, reach, step again, all very slowly, for several more minutes.

At last, with a final light jump, she was fully out into the wide corridor. There were no other meerkats to be seen in either direction, and all was silent. Which way should she go, however? She just had to hope that even if she came nowhere near the pups or Pebble, she would still find out something useful.

What did she risk? Being discovered as a spy for the Duwara instead of one of their victims, and being treated accordingly. That, as far as Slash was concerned, might involve some...well, slashing, Sheena was forced to accept.

Best not to get caught, then; so she moved as silently as she could, peering round corners before she actually went round them, sneaking a look into chambers before she passed by their entrances, and generally behaving as much like a spy as she could.

Remembering the horrible time she had had when she got lost

in the Deepden labyrinth, she took care to leave a light scratch in the sand whenever she came to a junction, so that she would be able to find her way back again.

She had not covered much ground when she detected movement ahead of her and to one side. It was coming from a passage that joined at right-angles the one she was moving carefully down. She slowed further, stepping gently in the soft sand so that she made no sound at all. She could hear a shuffling noise, and a soft, tight hiss as breath was expelled from the lungs of a creature that sounded thin, and long.

She feared it was a snake: after her previous encounters *with* snakes she was terrified *of* them.

There was more and louder hissing. The creature, whatever it was, was talking to itself. Sheena paused in mid-step and listened nervously, ready to run even if that meant pain as she undid the healing effect a day's rest had had on her wounds. She was worried that a snake would be able to slither through these narrow passageways more quickly than she could run, particularly in her weakened condition. She should not have been so eager to take up her spying duties, she decided: she should have been content to carry out her injured cat duties a little longer.

She began to hear what the creature was saying. The hissy words ran into each other as if they were all part of one very long, expelled breath of air, and she had to listen very carefully to sort them out from one another.

'ItsssclossseIsssmellitclossseitsssawarmanimalitsssnotameerkati tsssssananimalthatsssbeenlickedbymeerkatsssitsssananimalthatblee dsssmaybeIcanmakeitbleedsssomemore.'

A large scaley head suddenly poked out of the side tunnel, then shot back again.

'WhoopsssitsssquiteabiganimalandithasssclawssssssoIthinkIllw aituntilitssspasssedbyandssseewhereitgoesssandthengosssomewhe reelssse.'

Sheena had half-recognised the head; and now she thought about it the voice was familiar too. Not the exact head nor the exact voice; but a monitor lizard she had met on the school campus more than a year before had had a head, and a voice, very like these. It was that large brown lizard who had told Sheena about life in the wild and made her want to go on safari for the first time. Little did she know then how much amazement there was to be found in the world.

Sheena knew that monitor lizards were generally not aggressive unless they were attacked, at which point they became very aggressive indeed. She had no intention of attacking this one, so had nothing much to fear from it and might have something to gain. She stepped forward and looked sideways down the connecting passageway.

This was indeed a monitor. It was slimmer than the stocky, friendly specimen who had introduced himself as Kenge, and its markings were grey and white rather than brown and yellow, but it had the same general shape and the same beady black eyes. It also had the same bright blue tongue, sliding in and out from between its thin lips and waving about in the air as if it was looking for something. That was how it had known Sheena was there, and had learned so much about her: it could smell (very precisely) with its tongue.

Unlike Kenge, however (who had not wanted to be confused with a snake), this one made no attempt to control its hissing.

'SssalrighttheresssnothingtobessscaredofImjussstonmywayssso mewheresssojussstssstepasssideandIllgoaboutmybusssinesss.'

Sheena did not at all believe that this sneaky reptile was supposed to have *busssinesss* in Longburrow. What was it doing creeping around the tunnels in the middle of the night like a long thin puncture?

'Where is it that you're going, Kenge?'

Sheena thought she would try the same name on this lizard: perhaps all monitors were called Kenge. This one accepted it readily enough.

'OhImjussstgoingtofindsssomemeerkatpupsssthataresssleeping downheresssomewheremytonguewasssbusssysssmellingthemoutb utyoursssmellsssuddenlygotintheway.'

Could these possibly be the Duwara pups? If so, Pebble would probably be with them.

'How close do you think they are?'

'Clossseclossebutinasspecialplasssewhereothermeerkatsssarent sssupposssedtogoIllsssoonfindthemnoworriesss.'

'Why do you want to do that?'

Sheena thought she already knew the answer to her question.

'SssothatIcaneatthemofcourssseetheytassstesssosssweetwhenthe yresssmallandtheyresssocasssytocatwhentheyrehelplessss.'

Sheena needed to get in the way of that plan; but she also saw an opportunity here. Dad Allen had once talked about a tv interview in which a film actor had recalled some good advice his father had given him when he was younger: *Use the difficulty.* When a problem arose you should try to turn it to your advantage. Kenge was a difficulty: Sheena would use him.

'I wouldn't mind a nibble of pup myself,' she said. 'Would there by any chance be enough for both of us?'

'OnewillbesssufficientformeIvejussthadasssmallssnakeforsssta rtersthisssway.'

The monitor came forward into the tunnel Sheena was in, shuffling heavily on feet with long digging claws rather like meerkats', and turned down it in the direction she had been

153

travelling. He breathed noisssily as he walked.

Sheena followed watchfully, although all there was for her to watch was Kenge's scaley tail, swaying from side to side just off the tunnel floor. The lizard seemed to know his way through the system. Each time a passageway joined the one they were moving down he stopped, turned his head in the direction of the new opening, and flicked his tongue in and out several times. Sometimes he chose to go down the side-tunnel, sometimes not.

Sheena continued to leave scratches in the sand, surreptitiously now, whenever they entered a new tunnel.

Before long he took a sharp right turn, into a wider passageway. Right there in front of them was a pyramid of sleeping meerkats, reaching almost to the roof, with legs and tails flopping out in all directions. Most of the meerkats were slightly flattened by the weight of the ones above, and altogether the pyramid looked like a pile of warm pancakes. It didn't smell like one, however.

Luckily there was space round the outside of the pyramid, and a deal of snoring coming from inside it at different heights; so the lizard was able to creep around it without incident. Sheena followed, taking care not to touch any furry limbs.

The passageway beyond the pyramid was barred. There was a set of roots growing straight down through the roof and into the tunnel floor. Sheena did not remember seeing any trees near Heartmound, only a few large, scrubby bushes. One of those must have sent its roots down to this depth in search of water.

The roots were set quite closely together, but were pliant – they were more of a hindrance, or a warning, than a real obstruction. Kenge slipped through with no difficulty. Sheena had to force her much plumper body through the widest gap. The roots bent sufficiently to allow her to pass but straightened and closed again behind her. She would not be able to get out in a hurry, if that became necessary.

The tunnels here were mustier, and narrower: there was an unused, unvisited air about this section of Longburrow.

They went down a few more short lengths of tunnel, and took a few more turns.

Then she thought she heard noises. They had reached the entrance to a chamber. The sounds became clearer. They were a snuffling, and a breathing of meerkats, and an occasional faint whimper. Kenge had paused in the entrance. Sheena came alongside.

The three pups were there, in a huddle in one corner. Pebble was there, curled up by himself. A young female meerkat was fast asleep in the middle of the chamber. Spickle sat to one side, his bright eyes wide open, watching Sheena and the monitor.

Things happened very quickly. The monitor hissed loudly and lunged towards the pups. Sheena leapt forward and bit into his tail, half-way down where it was still quite thick. Kenge hissed again, even more loudly, and turned on her, his large mouth gaping. She had forgotten how many teeth there were in a monitor's mouth. Kenge was clearly capable of inflicting some serious wounds on her, to add to the injuries she had barely begun to recover from. She had stopped him temporarily, but something more permanent was necessary.

The female meerkat had woken up and was looking bewildered. Pebble had jumped to his feet and was obviously trying to work out what was happening. There was no time to explain anything. Sheena let go of Kenge's tail and whirled towards the chamber entrance. She skidded around the corner into the tunnel and set off to sprint back the way they had come, beginning to following the lines she had scratched in the tunnel floor. She could only hope that in his pain and rage the monitor would pursue her.

He did: his anger had overcome his hunger. She heard the shush of his claws in the sand as he gave chase, and his increasingly loud hissing as he began to catch up with her. She needed to outrun him only a little way: he would soon have more than her to deal with, if she managed to do what she intended.

She had forgotten the barrier of roots, however. She thudded into it and tried to force her way through, but in her haste she had not chosen the widest gap, and she was gripped and held by the springy growth. Then she felt her sore stump of a tail gripped as well, by the monitor's sharp teeth.

She managed to lodge her rear paws against the roots that were holding her, and pushed with all her might. That was enough to pull her rump through the gap, and the roots snapped back into place. Unfortunately for Kenge, his head happened to be just in the right place to be snapped back onto, and he let go of Sheena's tail. She ran. She ran towards the place where the meerkats were sleeping. Behind her she heard Kenge scrabbling through the roots and setting off after her once more.

Then she was at the meerkat pyramid. There was no sign of movement from it. She chose a tail sticking out near the bottom. It belonged to a meerkat who had already been half-squeezed out of the pile by the shifting weight of bodies above him. She sank her teeth into the tail, dug her paws into the sand and yanked hard.

The meerkat on the other end of the tail started to slide out backwards from the pile. He squealed loudly. The pyramid immediately began to totter, and became even more unstable as the rest of the animals jerked awake.

Sheena jumped back just in time to avoid falling bodies. The whole tower of meerkats crashed to the ground and they started running round in circles with their tails high in the air, not quite knowing what they were doing.

Kenge soon gave them a purpose. He arrived at speed, could not stop, and ran into the centre of the confusion. The meerkats' mad gyration now spun around him, then they swarmed over him, hissing, snapping and clawing, as if each one had a personal grievance against him that they badly wanted to settle. Perhaps Kenge hissed in response; but he could not be heard.

Sheena ran round the turmoil and down the wide passageway. She could do no more for the moment. She needed to get back to her own chamber, hope that the meerkats in their sleepy and befuddled state had not noticed her, and pretend that she had never been here.

Chapter Twenty: Kupanga

A little less than plain
If you take your eye off it,
But necessary
If you hope to profit.

Sheena wished she was as good at sleeping as her three guards, who had not stirred when she stepped carefully through them once more, back into the chamber. She spent the rest of the night awake, thinking about what had happened recently.

She now knew two things even more clearly than she had ever done before. Any animal (she was thinking of Tassel) could suddenly change the way it acted, and surprise you with opposites. And any animal in a species (now she had Kenge in mind) could behave very differently from other animals of the same kind.

Nothing in the behaviour of individual animals could be wholly relied on; and generalisations about whole groups so often did not hold true that they were hardly worth making.

She also, through the long hours, tried to decide how much if anything she had achieved by her little foray.

She had saved the life of at least one of the pups. She had also, at the same time, discovered where the pups and Pebble (and the unexpected Spickle) were being held – but what use would that knowledge be? She had little hope of being able to rescue them, and had not even been able to tell Pebble what she was doing there: he must be mightily puzzled.

She was very much afraid, also, that she had been seen by the meerkats from the pile, and recognised. Questions would now be asked. She waited fearfully for the formidable Slash to arrive at her chamber entrance.

He did not. Then it was morning once more, and she was taken up to the surface.

She was not at all unhappy to be on her way to Sunwatch. Being with meerkats at dawn, both here and at Deepden, had reminded her of how good it was when the sun showed itself for the first time each morning. In her younger life she had known that, and had forgotten.

Poor Pebble must be wasting away underground, deprived of a daily warming under the Duwara sun; would a warming under the Utongo sun have done him any good? And the pups – did they even know what a sun was? If the Utongo sun was the first they ever saw, would that make a difference to their lives, forever?

Sheena was held under guard at the foot of the mound, while the sun rose and everything else followed. It seemed she had been brought there not for her sake but so that Slash could interrogate her.

The large meerkat had perhaps been at Heartmound all night, and now showed no intention of going off on an inspection round (or even an inspection straight line). He was already on top of the mound, standing head and shoulders above the other meerkats. When the long moment of awakening was over the rest of the group jumped down and went about their business. So did the meerkats on all of the other mounds, Sheena noticed. Slash, however, stayed up on this mound, alone, turning his head this way and that, looking into the long distances. He obviously had much on his mind.

Eventually he leapt down to where Sheena was standing between her two guards.

She tried not to show her anxiety. This was the meerkat, no doubt, who had planned, and probably led, the attack on Deepden. What other wickedness might he be considering? This encounter would be tricky, and she would have to be at her trickiest.

He stood over her. His sharp eyes gleamed in the early sunlight, and seemed to look right into her once more.

Surprisingly, he said nothing about the events of the night. Had she not been spotted after all, then? Perhaps any meerkats who had glimpsed her as she raced off had thought she was part of whatever strange dreams they were having when the pile below was suddenly pulled from beneath them and the pile above came down round their ears. Perhaps the sight of an unwelcome monitor lizard in their midst, and the uproar that had followed, had emptied their minds of everything else.

'Well, cat,' said Slash. 'I am told that you were punished by the Duwara for failing.'

Sheena's disguise had held up, then. She said nothing.

'Tell me why you came to Longburrow.'

During the long night Sheena had also done some thinking in preparation for this inevitable question.

'I wanted to see your sun. The Duwara's sun seems to have had a bad effect on them. I think the Utongo sun may be a better one to live under.'

'You want to live here? What makes you think we will allow you to do that?'

'Well, I was hoping there might be a little corner somewhere that I might take up residence in for a while. I wouldn't need much space, and I travel quite a bit so you wouldn't see much of me.

'I don't mean in Longburrow itself of course – I'm an open-air creature. I just want to be able to see the sun at the beginning of each day, and settle down when I fancy in the shade of the trees, somewhere where I can look out onto the plain. I'd like to spend a few days in the area, now, and perhaps come back again some other time.'

Sheena was trying to make it clear that she had no wish for a permanent spot near Longburrow over which she might eventually claim squatter's rights. A lot of the problems between the Utongo and the Duwara seemed to be connected with territory, and she had no wish to get caught in the middle of that.

'If you'd rather I went further along The Gorge, it wouldn't much matter,' she continued, 'as long as I could stay on this side of it.

'I hear, by the way, you're hoping to move to the other side, yourselves – as well as continue to live on this side, of course.'

'Not *hoping* to move, *have* moved. We now control The Gorge. And we have an agreement to take over the place the Duwara call Rockhome. We shall call it Rockway.'

Agreement? That must be with Nungunungu. Perhaps Spickle's presence in Longburrow had something to do with it, in which case it might be an agreement Nungunungu hadn't been able to refuse. There were the pups also, and the demands that Shuffle had carried back to Deepden. The Utongo were obviously using hostages to get what they wanted.

'Why Rockway?'

Sheena was seeking confirmation of what she already suspected.

'Because it will be our way into Deepden, when the time is right.'

'Why into Deepden?'

'Because we need to make it ours. We need to drive out the Duwara. They have been corrupted by their sun.'

Sheena had to admit she was confused.

'Sorry – I don't understand. Won't you be corrupted too, if you go and live under their sun?'

'Ah, no. Our sun will follow us there, once we are established. It will drive out the false sun.'

('Oh!' thought Sheena.)

162

Slash suddenly spoke more grimly. 'Enough questions from you, however.'

(Was that because her questions were becoming a bit difficult to answer?)

'You are here to answer mine.'

Perhaps the rattle of his large claws at that point was accidental.

'How did the Duwara know we were going to attack them?' he demanded.

Sheena had to give him something.

'That Duwara meerkat you chased away from The Gorge, the one who walks with flat feet – he came back and told us…er, I mean them.'

She had to be careful not to let Slash see where her allegiances still lay.

But where did they now lie? She was not sure they were wholly with the Duwara. She was still thinking through the accusation that they had sent a sick meerkat to Longburrow.

'They had prepared cowardly traps for us,' said Slash, bitterly. 'We should have expected foul tricks like that. Some of the Utongo were badly injured. How did the Duwara think up such a device? They are not known for their cleverness.'

Sheena swallowed nervously. She had to be even more careful here.

'Oh, one of them sat on a porcupine quill when they settled down in one of the Rockhome chambers to discuss their defence of Deepden. That made him think – after it made him blink.'

'Ah, yes. We suspected Nungunungu helped them,' sad Slash, with cold anger.

'That is one reason why we have taken their offspring. They will not work against us now. In fact they will keep the Duwara out of Rockway, and will leave it themselves when we are ready to move there.'

'When will that be?'

'When our injured meerkats have recovered.'

Throughout this conversation, Slash had been stern but not aggressive; he had told Sheena more than she had told him; he had watched the young meerkats playing around them, and there had been a certain softening in his manner as he did so. Was he altogether as nasty a creature as Sheena had assumed? He seemed very upset at what he obviously saw as underhand behaviour by the Duwara.

Was taking hostages any better, however?

Several youngsters were tussling and rolling in twos and threes nearby, tail-biting and limb-twisting and neck-squeezing. One pair careened against Sheena's injured shoulder. She winced in pain.

'It would be best if you returned to your chamber with the Ndugu now,' said Slash. 'I will talk to you again soon.'

It seemed he had other things to attend to. That was not surprising, given what Sheena had learnt from him about the Utongo plans. The Duwara needed to be warned; but Pebble and the pups also needed to be protected, if they could not be rescued. There was too much here for one small cat to do!

Sheena followed Fade back down into the tunnel system. Tassel and Streak followed. Fade led them by a different route, and they arrived at a chamber with a young female meerkat and a single pup in it. The pup was feeding. Fade had come here to tell the nursing meerkat something. They did not stay there long – just long enough for Sheena to decide that one meerkat pup looked exactly like another.

'Whose pup is that?' she asked Tassel as they left. Spies were supposed to do that, she knew – gather information that would in all likelihood never be useful but might just.

'Its father is Slash. There were three in the litter…'

'…and the other two fell sick and died?' she guessed.

That might partly explain Slash's anger towards the Duwara.

'Yes, soon after they were born. And this one is not very strong.'

'But can Slash not have more pups?'

'Yes, in time; but he has too much to do now. He will not risk having more until we are victorious over the Duwara, and until he is certain there is no more disease among us; and he will first have to choose a new mate.

'His last one was called Sparkle. Her eyes were beautiful. Then the fever dulled them for ever.'

Sheena was beginning to have some unexpected sympathy with the Utongo, partly because of their surprising kindness towards her, partly because of the suffering the disease had brought them. Was her disguise, as an enemy of the Duwara and by implication therefore a friend of the Utongo, becoming a reality? Having moved from the tree to the ground as it were (like the chameleon), was she changing colour?

Half-way down the next tunnel they came to another, much larger chamber with a number of meerkats in it. Some were Ndugu Sheena had not seen before. They were tending to injured Utongo. Every now and again there was a whimper, as from a pup; but these were all fully-grown males.

Sheena was horrified to see the nature of their injuries. Most had been caused by porcupine quills. Some of the quills were still embedded in bodies and limbs, their barbs making it impossible for the Ndugu to get them out. One quill had gone clean through a meerkat's closed eyelid and into his eye. It still protruded, and the meerkat was lying sideways on the ground so that the weight of the quill was supported and its pulling would not cause him even greater suffering.

Goodness knew how these poor creatures had struggled back to Longburrow, carrying the instruments of their torture with them. Some of the injured must have perished in The Gorge; perhaps they were the lucky ones.

'This is what the Duwara have done. This is why we will be merciless.'

That was not the severe Slash talking: he was not there. It was not the changeable Tassel either, however, nor Streak. It was the gentle Fade, who had done so much to heal Sheena's wounds.

Sheena had been proud of her scheme to protect Deepden, and each Utongo scream in the night had even given her a little thrill. It had sounded like a victory.

Each one, however, had also meant that cruel pain had been inflicted on a meerkat, with perhaps death to follow. That was what was before her now in this awful place, and she could not look away.

It was at this point, confronted by so much suffering that she herself had caused in devising her Plan and persuading the Duwara to follow it, that Sheena thought up her *Grand* Plan.

Chapter Twenty-One: Ngangau

We can be spotted on all sides
When we're hunting in a clan.
We laugh at others' woes,
And cause more when we can.

She went on a sortie again that night. The pile of meerkats at her door was higher than it had been the night before, since there were four guards this time. (They did not include Tassel and Streak, who had left earlier.) She didn't think she was being trusted less, it was just that this foursome had chosen to fold themselves up in sleep together.

As a result, however, it took her a little longer to get out into the tunnel, and in the process she stood on a paw and an ear. The only response in each case was a sleepy squeak.

Sheena could now navigate underground much more easily, even without using the marks she had left the last time she had travelled this route. It was as if some long-unused skill had come back to her.

It did not take her long to reach the large pyramid of meerkats – not necessarily the same ones. They were of course fast asleep. They must have assumed that lizards don't strike twice in the same place.

There was a fishy sort of odour mingling with the meerkat smell. Had Kenge been killed (or worse still left half-alive) and just pushed aside to rot in a side-tunnel?

She crept around the meerkats. There was nary a twitch from the pile, and not a single eye opened. She came to the barrier of roots blocking off the quarantine area, wriggled through them and made her way to the chamber.

She was in the chamber for some time. When she left she brought with her more than she had intended. First there was Pebble, apparently recovered from his Kisusuli sting and suffering only from a lack of sunshine. Then there was Spickle. Sheena needed him as part of her Plan, but he would have refused to stay behind in any case – in fact Sheena had great difficulty in stopping him from running on in front.

Finally there was the young female. She had been given the job of feeding the Duwara pups as a punishment. If the pups had turned out to be carrying the disease (she had called it Duwara Fever) and she had caught it – well that would have been a part of the punishment, she had been told.

She had apparently broken a major rule of the tribe. Only Slash and his partner were allowed to breed. Other females who had pups were in danger of seeing them killed.

'Where are your pups now?' Pebble asked.

'Dead,' the young female replied; but she would not say how they had died. Perhaps it had been from Duwara Fever; but perhaps…

Pebble had told her that she herself would never have been punished so severely by the Duwara. She was clearly in fear of further ill treatment: at best she would rank very low in the tribe, and might eventually be cast out from it altogether, to live a lonely and vulnerable life drifting around its edges.

Deepden sounded to her, now, a better place to be than

Longburrow. As soon as she knew Sheena intended to lead Pebble and Spickle back to Deepden, she had asked to come with them.

She had only gone to the chamber, in fact, to make contact with Pebble and prepare him for what she intended to do soon – perhaps as soon as the next night. As they talked, however, it became clear that there was no good reason for not acting now. What had settled things was an offer made by the young female, Sift: it made the first part of the Plan suddenly seem more possible.

'We must go quickly, then,' said Sheena.

'Let's go quickly,' said Spickle.

They did not take the pups. Pebble was concerned about that; but Sheena explained why it had to happen. It would have been extremely difficult to carry them all; and in any case it was part of her Grand Plan to leave them behind.

The young female reassured Pebble that another Utongo female would be found to feed them. (Sheena did wonder in passing what effect it might be having on Duwara pups to be fed Utongo milk.) They would not be there for long, however: a very recent modification to the Plan would see to that.

They were soon through the barrier of roots (although the well-rounded little Spickle did get his spines caught in it when he changed his mind about which gap to go through and tried to back out to try another one).

When they reached the meerkat pyramid, things very nearly went more seriously wrong. As they crept quietly around the pile, as close to the side of the tunnel as they could get, Spickle's longer quills brushed the earth wall. Even though there were now only four of them they rattled slightly. A meerkat with his head

170

poking out of the pyramid unexpectedly stirred and opened a sleepy eye, then opened it wider when he saw the sharp spines waving just in front of his nose. Luckily Sift was just behind Spickle. She quickly stepped forwards and licked the meerkat's head, soothingly. He went back to sleep.

They reached the Utongo nursery where Sheena had seen the single pup. This was when Sift would really become useful.

She went towards the nursery. Sheena, Pebble and Spickle turned down a side tunnel and stayed out of sight. If what Sift had suggested worked, they would all be able to leave quietly. Otherwise they would be departing in a major hurry, probably with angry Utongo on their various (and variously shaped) tails.

It was doubtful whether Spickle wholly understood what was happening, but he made a good show of pretending.

There was a pause, and a silence. Then they heard a meerkat heading back down the tunnel towards them. They stayed back out of sight.

Sift appeared, carrying the single Utongo pup carefully in her mouth. Its body drooped peacefully on either side of her lower jaw, behind her sharp canine teeth. Its eyes were still closed: it was very young, too young to do anything other than trust, and sleep.

They chose to leave the tunnel system by the nearest exit, and travel to The Gorge over open ground. There was always some slight risk of meeting an almost-awake meerkat in the tunnels. Sift was sure they would not come across any of the Utongo outside, awake or asleep.

It seemed none of the exits was guarded. Meerkats apparently thought the world came to a halt when the sun went down, and there was therefore nothing much to worry about in the hours of darkness. This was in spite of the occasional problems they had at night with creatures like monitor lizards; and had they already forgotten their own night-time attack on Deepden? Did meerkats have two brains, like chameleons, and could one brain ignore what the other one knew?

They travelled only a short distance underground, then Sift led them out of Longburrow into the stillness of the night.

They soon reached the edge of the Gorge and set off along it, planning to turn down into its depths only when they reached the beginning of the easy route.

Then they began to hear the sounds. They came from some distance away, but also from different directions – a whooping noise, then from time to time a chuckling as if the animals making them were amused at something.

Sheena thought she recognised the calls.

'Hyenas.'

It was very unnerving, since it was as if the hyenas knew all about this mixed little group of animals making its way along The Gorge, and would soon close in on them and render their attempt at a journey futile, laughing (as laughing hyenas do) all the while.

Hyenas were both cowardly and ferocious beasts, Sheena knew – cowardly when they were in any danger, ferocious when they felt safe and hungry. These ones would not hesitate to make whatever meal they could out of two helpless meerkats and a very minor cat. They might think twice about putting their powerful jaws around the spiky ball that Spickle would become if they tried.

All the travellers could do was travel on. Pebble took the lead to begin with. There was a new moon, a delicate curve of silver light scratched as if with the finest of needles into the dark blue sky. It was beautiful, and Sheena wondered briefly whether it was possible to take strength from the moon, if you believed strongly enough that you could.

They made surprising speed: Sift seemed to have no difficulty carrying the pup, and Spickle kept up well, his little legs trotting along beneath his round body with a certain jerkiness as if he were a wind-up toy. There was no sound of pursuit from Longburrow behind, but there was always Longburrow ahead to worry about: they would need to pass quite close to The Gorge Tunnel entrance.

It took a long time for the hyenas to draw closer. By then Pebble was showing signs of exhaustion, and had dropped back among the group. His body obviously still held traces of Kisusuli poison.

The circle of whoops and giggles tightened around them, and they could hear heavy paws thudding on the sandy earth. Sheena began to see shapes lumbering past in the darkness, clumsy shapes with sloping backs moving at a slow and awkward gallop.

They had no protection. The hyenas began running directly in at them, then at the last minute veering off to one side. This was their way of checking that there was no animal in the group capable of hurting them. They were still in their cowardly mode, but would soon switch to their ferocious one.

The fleeing animals would have to take refuge; but the vegetation alongside which they were now running was too dense and thorny to allow them in.

The only other place they could hide was in The Gorge Tunnel entrance to Longburrow. The embankment lay ahead, across their path.

Sift now moved out in front, since she knew exactly where the entrance was. Spickle followed her, then Pebble and lastly Sheena. They had to climb up a slope before they got to the embankment, which slowed them down (Spickle's short legs weren't made for climbing, and neither Sheena nor Pebble felt like giving him a push from behind) but they eventually reached the tunnel and hurried inside, with the pounding of paws right behind them.

Sheena immediately turned and faced the entrance, determined to do what she could to keep the hyenas at bay. It would be a contest between sharp claws and terrible jaws; but she was at an enormous disadvantage because of the hyenas' much greater size and strength, not to mention their numbers – there were four of them, now charging in turn at the tunnel mouth, stopping just short and turning away, all the while cackling, whooping, and drooling in anticipation of food.

At last one of them came all the way, and jammed his large square head into the mouth of the tunnel. His broad shoulders would not let him crawl any further in. Sheena was just out of reach. His eyes were red and fiery, his big teeth yellow in the darkness. Slaver hung glistening from his lower jaw. Sheena could smell the foulness of his breath: he had been chewing putrid meat.

His voice was loud, and he spoke with a triumphant rhythm which filled the tunnel.

> '**No**where to **go**, **no**where to **hide**,
> *You can* **stay** *where you* **are** *but we'll* **soon** *be in***side***.'*

He ended his little rhyme with a cruel cackle, and pulled his head back out of the hole to grin horribly at the other hyenas, who had sat down in a half-circle outside and now responded with whoops and gurgles. They apparently liked entertainment, and thought they were about to get some, with refreshments at the end. They started some chanting of their own, in chorus.

> '**We're** N**gang***au*, *ugly yet* **cute**,
> *We* **like** *to have* **fun***, we* **think** *life's a* **hoot**.'

The lead hyena stuck his head back into the hole continued his taunting.

*'We've got **plenty** of **time** to **dig** you **out**,*
*Then it's **munches** all **round** without a **doubt**.'*

These creatures seemed to delight in measured mockery, accompanied by wild background whooping.

'I thought raptors were a kind of bird,' Sheena said to herself.

Would they be able to dig into the passageway with their broad paws more quickly than Sheena and the others could retreat down it? Probably not; but the tunnel led back into Longburrow, where they did not want to go. Perhaps, however, they could pretend to the hyenas that they were returning there, disappear down the tunnel and wait until the hyenas left. She would prepare the way for that. She spoke as jauntily as she could.

*'**Don't** be so **sure**, **maggot mouth**.*
***You're** sitting **North** and **we're** heading **South**.'*

The reply was quick to come.

*'**Seems** to **us** you've **run** away.*
*You **can't** go **back** so you're **here** to **stay**.'*

The rest of the hyenas hooted loudly. Perhaps they were all smarter than their slobber suggested.

Sheena was standing on all fours at her full height, blocking the tunnel and trying to look as big as possible. She suddenly had a curious sensation beneath her stomach, as if someone was drawing a comb through her fur in the wrong direction, just as Thomas did when he was checking her for fleas. Spickle was crawling forward underneath her, and his pointed nose soon poked out between her front legs. She had a momentary fear that he would jam her in the tunnel like he had jammed Nungu, and make her easy prey for the hyena if he chose to reach in with his thick claws. She tried a little backwards shift and found she could slide easily over Spickle's spines. He, however, would not be able to retreat without puncturing her.

He had no plans to retreat. He had his own little ditty to offer.

*'Don't **like** big **teeth**, don't **like** big **paws**,*
*Don't **like** big **noses**, so here's **something for yours**.'*

With that he stalked fully out from beneath Sheena and raised his sharp little spines. Then he suddenly spun round and jabbed his whole body backwards into the hyena's face.

He was only copying what he had seen his much larger father do; but his attack was very effective in the narrow confines of the tunnel, which allowed the hyena no room to lift his head out of the way. Spickle might have only a few quills, but the longest of them sank very smoothly into the hyena's wet nose.

That was not an entirely good result. His quills, since he was young and they were quite new, did not pull out at all easily at his end; at the sharp end, however, they were already barbed, and did not pull out at all. The one he had jabbed into the hyena stayed firmly attached to Spickle's own skin, so when the hyena yelped loudly and jerked backwards in pain, Spickle was yanked tail-first out of the hole.

For a brief moment he dangled head-down from the hyena's nose, several inches off the ground. Then the hyena batted him downwards with a weighty paw. Spickle was knocked onto the hard earth. 'Ow!' he said, as the quill of which he had been proudest was plucked from his back.

It was still firmly fixed in the hyena's soft flesh, however. He backed off violently, as if that would take him away from the source of the pain; then he shook his head and pawed at the embedded spine, yelping some more.

Spickle, as he landed, instinctively curled himself up into a ball. The momentum of his fall carried him forward, and he rolled towards the other hyenas. They had not quite grasped what was happening, and thought this round object trundling towards them was part of the entertainment. One of them danced to one side and gave it a hard whack from behind with a front paw as if it was a football and he was trying to pass it to one of his companions. He yelped just as loudly as the first hyena had done: one of Spickle's remaining quills had driven deep into the soft pad behind his claws, and the speed of the little porcupine's forwards roll plucked the spine free from his own body, leaving it dangling from the paw the hyena, now whining, held up in the air

The remaining two hyenas had by now realised that Spickle was not a creature to be played with, and jumped aside, allowing him to roll on down the slope.

Sheena saw an opportunity to strike a blow of her own. The two hurt hyenas continued to yelp and whine, one pulling with his teeth at the spine in his paw, the other pawing at the spine in his nose. The uninjured pair were standing with their backs to the tunnel entrance, watching Spickle roll away from them. Sheena ran out and sank her teeth into the back of the nearest hyena's ankle. She knew that was a very sensitive area (the Achilles tender, she thought she had heard Dad Allen call it).

It was this hyena's turn to yelp. He whirled around to bite her, but she was no longer there: she was already half-way back into the tunnel, singing out over her shoulder.

> '*The* **foot** *is* **in** *the other* **shoe***:*
> **Life's** *a* **hoot** *but the* **joke's** *on* **you.**'

Three out of four hyenas were now hurt; and that was an unsettling percentage as far as the fourth one was concerned. He sloped off (a very good word for a hyena). The others immediately followed, whining and walking in funny ways.

Chapter Twenty-Two: Sungusungu

We journey on a million legs,
Guarding our flanks with jaws of steel.
We can drink deep from a drop of rain
But of the largest animal make a meal.

Sheena told Pebble and Sift to stay in the tunnel while she ran down the slope to find Spickle. She wondered how far he might have rolled.

She need not have been concerned. He met her when she was half-way down the slope, his short legs working hard to bring him back up towards the tunnel entrance.

'Those were my two best quills,' he said, somewhere between sadly and proudly.

'I've only got two left now. I'd better chew some bones soon.'

He had an opportunity to do just that before they had travelled very far into The Gorge. It was still dark. They needed to stop and rest, but realised they could not rest long. When Longburrow awoke to the new day the Utongo would know where they had gone, and Slash would know that they had taken his pup with them. He would give furious chase.

That was part of Sheena's Grand Plan, of course, to bring Slash back through The Gorge to Deepden; another part was to make sure that before he arrived the Duwara had something to bargain with. The return of Spickle and Pebble would help restore the balance of power between the two warring tribes. Balance was important throughout nature, Sheena knew, whether you were just jumping from a tree to a wall or doing something on a larger scale like trying to get along with your neighbours. The Utongo had lost two of their hostages: they would not be able to use Pebble as a means of exerting pressure on the Duwara, and could now no longer rely on Nungunungu to hand Rockhome over to them. More importantly, each tribe would hold the newest offspring of the other's leaders.

'*Then* they'll *have* to talk,' said Sheena to herself.

She needed to lead the group safely through The Gorge first. She felt she would be able to find the way without much trouble: down one side and up the other shouldn't be too difficult. She was revisited by the feeling she had had previously, however, that there were more terrible things in the depths of The Gorge than she had encountered the first time.

They stopped just past the first line of trees. Pebble, suffering more and more from the lingering effects of the scorpion sting, was having difficulty keeping up. Sift was exhausted, having carried the pup all this way by herself. She also needed to feed it. She laid it gently on the ground and licked it awake. It mewed (more like a kitten than a pup, Sheena thought). Spickle complained about the sore spots where his quills had been pulled out; but nobody offered to lick *them*.

After a short while Pebble roused himself, weak though he was, and began to sniff and snuffle in the soft earth, looking for food. Sheena tried too, but her short nose was not designed for rooting out grubs. They were soon joined by Sift, who was much better at the task than either of them. She demonstrated how she had got her name: she seemed to have developed her own grub-gathering technique, and it was very effective. She clawed into the sandy soil to soften it, then scooped it up and let it trickle out slowly between her claws. She closed her claws on any small wriggling things left in her palm, and passed them round to the others.

Then she returned to the pup and allowed it to feed again. She treated it very tenderly, Sheena noticed, and lay curled around it even after it had stopped feeding and fallen asleep once more. Had it begun to replace in her life at least one of the pups she had lost?

'Does it have a name yet?' Sheena asked.

'No. It must be old enough to join us in Sunwatch first of all. Then we will wait to see what is special about it. That will help us to think of a name. But Slash will decide, in the end. He is its father.'

The meerkat talked as if they were still back in Longburrow, where Slash was in charge and Sunwatch happened every morning. All of that might now have changed for her, permanently.

As soon as they stopped Spickle had gone off by himself to find food. He came back now with a long worm curling out of both sides of his mouth. After he had bitten it in half and sucked the two halves down he found a pile of greying bones at the foot of a tree and began to gnaw one of them, noisily.

'Just watch my quills grow!' he said happily.

Sheena looked, but the short spines covering most of his body showed no sign of getting any longer. He would have to make do with his remaining quills for a while to come.

'Sorry — we can't wait for that to happen,' she said. 'We must move on.'

'We must move on,' said Spickle firmly, as if it was his idea.

Sheena led them carefully down into the depths of The Gorge. Sift had difficulty on the steepest slopes: the pup swinging in her mouth made it difficult for her to place her front paws with enough care, and Pebble went in front of her in case she started to slide out of control. Sheena had to stop Spickle setting off on one of his rolls.

They were about half-way down, on a level piece of ground, when they began to hear a rustling all around them. It was not coming from the trees but from the earth, and from the small plants that grew there and the leaves scattered among them. What grass there was began to shake, and the leaves started to tremble and shift, as if a tide of water was sweeping in through them, on all sides.

Then the tide rose through the grass and leaves, and showed itself to be a sea of black ants, pouring towards them over the ground, over the lowest of the vegetation, then over Spickle, who had taken a slightly different path off to one side.

'Sungusungu!' said Pebble in horror.

It was as if everything at ground level, including Spickle, was being submerged in a dark flow of hot tar, melting into it and disappearing.

It must have felt something like that, too, for the little porcupine. He suddenly started to squeak in pain as the ants found their way down between his spines and bit him viciously. He curled up in a ball, but that simply trapped ants inside, close to his skin. He rolled forward, impaling several ants on the points of his shorter spines; but there were far too many of them. Soon it was hard to see him under the swarming mass. He could still be heard, however, squealing pitifully.

The others could do nothing to rescue him. The black flood swept at them and over them, and immediately they too were in agony. Each of the many thousands of safari ants attacking them had a formidable pair of jaws – so powerful, Sheena knew, that local people used them instead of stitches to hold deep wounds closed: they allowed the ants to bite into their flesh and then nipped off their heads so that the jaws stayed in place and kept the two sides of the wound together until it had healed.

That wasn't all: as they closed their jaws on a victim, the ants delivered a painful shot of acid. An animal bitten often enough would fall and be devoured. The ants could then strip it to the bone, in no time. The pup could not survive long, but none of them would survive much longer.

Sift spoke with difficulty: the ants had swarmed over the pup and entered her mouth.

'This way...that tree...'

Sheena strained to look through her half-closed eyes and past the ants hanging from her eyelids, biting, biting. There was a small tree a little distance away, with closely-packed dark-green leaves. Surely climbing a tree would not help: ants could easily swarm up tree-trunks. In any case, it did not look very climbable – it was not much more than a large shrub.

Sift, however, led the way towards it, and the three others followed, carrying a weight of ants, wading through a depth of others, struggling to see where they were going, helping each other as much as they could. The pain got worse all the time, as the amount of acid in their bodies increased. They could feel their burning flesh beginning to swell. Soon they would not be able to see out of their eyes at all. Ants had crawled into their throats, and the bites from those were causing their airways to narrow, making it difficult to breathe.

Then they reached the tree. Sift did not pause but plunged straight in amongst its leaves, which grew close to the ground. They all followed. Through their nostrils, half-blocked by ants, they could smell a very pungent odour. Sheena thought it was like a mixture of diesel fumes, honey and lion musk (which she remembered well) – a heavy, sickly, drowsy sort of smell.

Miraculously, the biting lessened, then stopped, and clumps of ants began to drop from their bodies to the bare earth beneath the tree. Some crawled away, but most lay where they fell, either in a stupor or dead. No ants had followed them in amongst the leaves. It was as if they had swum to an island in the middle of a dark and angry sea, and had been saved from a dreadful drowning.

They themselves felt drowsy, either from the heady fumes or from the poison in their flesh. They lay down, and passed into unconsciousness, while the pain slowly ebbed out of their bodies.

Chapter Twenty-Three: Wazazi

Once we had some
Just like us,
And to them we were
Equally precious.

They woke with difficulty, much later. It was Sift who roused the others.

'Must leave here…stay too long…sleep for ever.'

It seemed the fumes from the trees were dangerous in their own way, and they all needed to get out into the fresh air before it was too late. They dragged themselves up into full consciousness. Sheena knew she had been having very strange and powerful dreams, but could not remember about what.

Their pain, and their swelling, had gone. Apart from the bodies of innumerable ants under the tree, only the memory of the nightmare remained. They looked carefully out from among the leaves to make sure that it *was* only a memory, and that their little island was not still surrounded by the sea of vicious sungusungu. (In her dreamy state, Sheena wondered momentarily about the Kiswahili name for safari ants. Would the ants have the same problem as multiple Nungunungu and, when they were being talked about as a whole group, need to be called Sungusungusungusungusungusungusungu, over the horizon?)

Everything was still, and not a single live ant could be seen.

While they slept, day had arrived, but only in the form of a general greyness among the trees.

They crept out and took deep breaths of clear air, trying to rinse their minds free of sleepiness and confusion.

They found the trek down to the bottom of The Gorge difficult: they were still unsteady on their feet, and their reactions were slow. Sift slipped badly, twice. The second time Pebble tried to help her, but was too slow, and she fell heavily among some rocks, dropping the pup and landing partly on top of it. It squeaked loudly, but only briefly. Once Spickle tripped, and dived nose-first into a roll that carried him a long way down the slope then, finally and with a loud crash, into some bushes. Sheena suspected it might have been deliberate: he was not finding this long walk enjoyable, even though for him it was a walk home. By the time they got down to where he was, he was asleep and had to be woken again.

Sheena was relieved when they neared the dry stream bed, even though Sift had to be helped down the last few rocky levels (Spickle just curled up again and bounced down). They sank into the deep drifts of sand right at the bottom of The Gorge, struggled free and began the long climb upwards.

It was soon after that that they heard the sounds of what could only be pursuit – loose stones rattling down the Utongo side of The Gorge, the occasional scrabbling of paws, and then meerkat voices drifting directly to them across the steep valley.

Slash and his party would be travelling much more swiftly than Sheena and hers. They struggled on and up, through the rocks and round the rocks when they could, up the rocks when they had to. They were soon very tired, and they could now hear their pursuers below them on this side of the valley.

The ground levelled out somewhat, and the going became

easier. They would not have that advantage for long: they heard the quick patter of paws below. The Utongo were catching up fast.

'Hell*ooo*,' said Mondo.

'I was *hoping* you would come back this way for a re-match.'

Sheena had not noticed the serval cat lying along a high, flat rock with just the top of her head showing. As she spoke she rose to her full height, did her languorous stretching once more, and leapt down gracefully onto the flat piece of ground where Sheena, the meerkats and Spickle now stood. She looked down at them superciliously.

'Are you all hoping to go through here? We'll have to see. I'm not sure I can issue a group pass.'

Pebble and Sift did not know quite what to make of Mondo, beyond the fact that her smooth manner seemed also threatening. Sheena was initially worried – Mondo clearly saw herself as a kind of gatekeeper, with the authority to stop passers-through, and also as the local slashing champion…but that last thought gave Sheena an idea. She would use the difficulty.

'I'm glad we've found you. I've brought my friends to watch you perform,' she said. She thought *perform* would appeal to Mondo's vanity.

'O good! Shall we make it first to twenty this time? I found that last bout rather short – I didn't have time to warm up properly.'

'No, no, I didn't mean perform with *me*,' said Sheena. 'I'm no real competition for you. I just got confused last time and went the wrong way – sorry about that.

'I've brought a real challenger. He's called Slash, and he's got the fastest claws on the far side of The Gorge. He's just behind, with some of his fans.'

'Oh, well, fine.'

Mondo spoke confidently.

'You and I can get together some other time.'

No thanks, Sheena thought. What she said was, 'We'll just climb up here, then, and watch, if that's alright.'

Sheena led the others up onto the rock where Mondo had been lying, and then beyond it so they were further up the slope and amongst some vegetation.

'Oh by the way,' she called back down, 'Slash is very proud of his stamina. If you really want to prove you're better than him, you'd better make it first to fifty.'

They waited only long enough to see the tall figure of Slash arrive. He was accompanied by five other meerkat males, probably chosen for their swiftness and fighting prowess.

'Welcome. I'm Mondo,' said the serval, simply, just as she had to Sheena. She clearly assumed the band of meerkats would know how important she was. She had jumped back up onto the flat rock to emphasise that importance.

The Utongo stopped.

'I don't care who you are.' Slash's voice was angry, and his teeth were showing.

'We need to pass. We are Utongo.'

Mondo was firmly in their way.

'That's the spirit!' she said. 'I like a bit of role-play. And I like the teeth – well done. You should shout and stamp as well, though. The spectators like it, you know, even if it's only pretend. And show your claws. What about a bit of hissing and a glare or two?'

Slash was stamping and hissing, and showing his claws, before Mondo had finished; but it wasn't pretend.

Sheena, Pebble and Sift had sunk down almost out of sight as

189

soon as this exchange began. Neither Slash nor his companions noticed the three heads among the bushes above the rock (Spickle hadn't been able to lift his high enough to see); and Mondo, who had her back to them, did not see the fugitives as they disappeared.

Disappear they did, quickly. As they turned and began to climb the slope again, they heard sudden movement, then Mondo's casual drawl.

'Three-nil to me.'

Sheena knew what had happened; the others could only guess.

They made all possible speed up the rest of The Gorge's steep slopes. If Mondo pressed home her advantage (part of which might lie in the fact that she probably hadn't fully explained her rules to Slash) then the contest could be over quite quickly. Then according *to* her rules Slash at least would not be able to pass. The other meerkats were unlikely to want to advance without him; and in any case, if they tried, Mondo would have something to say about that...and Sheena was sure she was quite capable of fighting off all of them if she had to.

She found herself hoping, however, that Slash would not be too badly hurt.

As they neared the top of The Gorge Sheena thought she saw, on a patch of bare ground off to one side, a large stone with a moving eye, watching them. She did not have time to investigate.

There were no sounds of a chase behind them when they broke through onto the Duwara side of The Gorge and saw, in the distance, the welcome sight of Rockhome dark against the sandy plain. Spickle immediately began to run (a stumpy trot was the best he could manage) and Sheena did not try to stop him. If the Utongo somehow managed to get past Mondo, they would all have to run, and Spickle would be the slowest of them.

She and the two meerkats had not moved very far into the open when Pebble stopped and stood up on his hind legs, facing the sun. It was well past sunrise, and its rays were hot. He seemed to go immediately into a kind of trance. Sheena was about to urge him onwards, then she realised that he needed this. He had not seen any sunshine at all for several days; and this was his own sun, the Duwara sun.

Sift had stopped also, and laid the pup down on the ground. It did not move. She looked up fearfully at the bright disc more than half-way up the sky.

'Your sun is very strange,' she said. 'It seems smaller than the Utongo sun, but brighter, and less kind. It is hot but it makes me feel cold inside. I cannot stay out here long, I must reach a burrow soon, or go back to the trees. Help me, please.'

There was a note of panic in her voice.

There was no burrow nearby, and returning to the trees was not an option. Sheena was becoming anxious. She thought she could hear meerkat noises at the edge of The Gorge.

Sift hesitated, then said, 'I will travel on; but we must hurry.'

She picked up the pup and they began to run once more. They had no sooner caught up with Spickle, a little more than half-way to Rockhome, than they heard angry growling and hissing from the trees behind them. As they turned to look, the Utongo burst out from the undergrowth and began racing after them across the flat plain. Sheena did not know how they could have got past Mondo. Slash was at the front. Sheena thought she could see bloodstains on his fur, and maybe on some of the other meerkats' as well.

What followed should have been a simple race; but nothing involving Spickle was simple. Not only was he slower than the others because of his short legs, his short legs kept getting mixed up, and several times he tripped and rolled and had to straighten himself out, get up and begin running again. Sometime he got up and began running again before he had straightened himself out, and immediately fell once more.

Sheena stayed with him. She could probably have outpaced the meerkats, but she knew Spickle would become important to them all, very soon.

Pebble and Sift reached Rockhome together, well ahead of

Sheena and Spickle. They disappeared inside. Sheena and Spickle got closer to the entrance. The Utongo got closer to Sheena and Spickle. Slash was ahead of the other meerkats, and before long right on Sheena's heels. Sheena ran close behind Spickle, hoping that he would not stop suddenly.

Slash had little interest in either her or Spickle, however: he was simply trying to get in front of them both so that he could run swiftly through the tunnels and catch up with Pebble and Sift before they carried his pup into the more secure parts of Deepden.

The other Utongo, however – they might turn nasty if they got their paws on Sheena and (carefully, to be sure) on Spickle.

In his eagerness Slash did something Sheena had not seen any of the meerkats do so far. He leapt – over her first of all, into the space between her and Spickle, and then, in another bound, over Spickle. He would reach Rockhome ahead of them.

He did not even get as far as the entrance, however. He came face to face with Nungu instead.

Spickle's father suddenly appeared between the rocks. He was facing forward and his dangerous quills were behind him, but he still looked fearsome. His teeth were small, but they were bared. His claws were long. He bristled.

'No!' he said, angrily.

'No Utongo enter Rockhome.'

Two just have, Sheena thought; but it was Slash and his group that Nungu had set his face against. They were the ones who had taken Spickle by force. Then he set his quills against them too, turning swiftly and backing towards Slash, and also the rest of the Utongo, who by now had arrived at the pile of rocks.

Nungu was some way forward from the cave entrance. Sheena was quick to dodge around both him and Slash and run towards the cave. She assumed Spickle would follow her, but she should have known better. He turned round and lined up with his father, his quills (what was left of them) pointing backwards as threateningly as he could manage.

'No Utongo enter Rockhome,' he said.

For a moment it seemed as if Nungu's move might have been a bad one, and Spickle's hardly any better. The meerkats spread out and began to encircle both porcupines, the large and the small. They would be able to get between them and Rockhome, and either attack their less protected fronts or simply run on into the tunnels.

Then Nungu suddenly appeared in the tunnel entrance. She stalked out, as angry-looking as Nungu and almost as large.

'Go inside!' she growled at Spickle.

'But...' he said.

'Let him stay!' said Nungu.

So Spickle held his ground in the centre between his parents. His father had half-turned towards him and his mother took up a similar position on his other side, so that they were all three facing towards the cave entrance, in a semi-circle and with their quills pointing back out towards the Utongo. Sheena found herself protected by something like a prickly thorn hedge, with the meerkats hopping and hissing outside it, helplessly.

The three porcupines then slowly closed in, nose first, towards the tunnel entrance. All Sheena had to do was turn and run inside, ahead of them. Spickle followed her, then Nungu, then Nungu – who stopped as soon as the entrance narrowed, and raised his spines until they blocked the tunnel from floor to roof and side to side. They were all safe.

Chapter Twenty-Four: Tembo Mpole

On both sides I can flap,
At both ends I can swish.
In between I move slowly,
But more quickly when I wish.

Thomas had talked once about a book he had had to read at school. It was about two groups of people who went to war over the question of which end of a soft-boiled egg you should crack open, the round end or the pointed end.

It seemed to Sheena that these wars over which of two suns was better were just as absurd.

There was only one sun in the sky. She knew she had had momentary doubts about that (all the meerkats seemed so convinced there were two) but had come back to the firm belief that the sun was the sun wherever you saw it from. If she could persuade the meerkats of that fact, it would bring to an end all of this nonsense about one tribe being better than the other because it lived under the only 'true' sun. As far as Sheena could see the Utongo and the Duwara were as bad, and as good, as each other. She wanted them to realise that; so she had to settle the argument about the sun.

How could she do so, however?

That question had been the starting point of her Grand Plan; bringing Slash and Tuft together was the first step; and that was why things were now as they were.

They were only at a beginning. Slash and Tuft had never met, as far as Sheena knew. What might happen when they did?

Pebble and Sift had kept going as fast as they could, once they were in the tunnel leading from Rockhome, not knowing that it was going to be so effectively blocked, behind them, against the Utongo.

Nungunungu had been resting in one of their side chambers near the tunnel entrance when the two meerkats ran in and past, and had been taken by surprise. Nungu had chased after them a little way while Nungu went to see what was happening in front of the den, but a mother's sixth sense had called her back to join him outside. Nungunungu had been delighted to see Spickle, and angered to see him apparently under threat from the Utongo. So they had acted.

Spickle could not wait to tell his parents about the encounter with the hyenas, and his part in it. Sheena felt he deserved a compliment, so she came up with a tongue-twister like the ones she had made up on her first visit to Baragandiri.

'The unexpected Spickle sticks trickily with his prickly spines,' she said to Nungunungu. Spickle liked that, and began repeating it to himself to see how quickly he could say it without making a mistake. He fell over the words, however, as easily as he had fallen over his feet when he tried to run too fast.

Nungunungu were clearly very proud of him. No doubt much nuzzling would go on, but Sheena wasn't sure quite how porcupines managed that safely.

She could not stay to see. She badly needed to catch up with Pebble and Sift. Pebble must smell of Utongo, and Sift and the pup *were* Utongo: the Duwara might kill all three without hesitation unless she was there to stop them.

She was just in time. She came to a fork in the tunnel. She could see Pebble's tail disappearing down the left-hand branch; and coming towards her at great speed down the right-hand one was Stab, with several other meerkats behind him. Pebble must have heard them and taken Sift off in a different direction.

'Out of our way!' Stab snarled.

Sheena willingly stepped aside into the tunnel Pebble and Sift had run down, screening what was left of them from view. Stab led his group onwards without pausing, in the direction of Rockhome.

Sheena took up the chase again, and before long saw Pebble's long tail waving ahead of her as he continued to run.

'Wait! It's alright! The Utongo have been stopped!' she called.

'It's not alright,' Pebble said, stopping and turning to her. 'Their pup is dead.'

Sift had laid the pup gently on the ground, and was licking it slowly. They had to give her time.

She was sure the pup had died because it had been exposed to the Duwara sun.

'I think I would have died too, if I had been out there much longer,' she said.

Sheena thought it much more likely that the pup had died from Sungusungu bites, or that it had been more badly injured than they realised when Sift fell. She did not say that to Sift.

This part of her plan was not working at all well. Slash's hatred of the Duwara would increase when he heard about the death of his pup, even though the Duwara were not at all responsible for it, and he might wreak a terrible revenge. If he could not do so here, he certainly would when he got back to Longburrow.

The situation had changed in more ways than that, however.

Sheena discovered as much when they reached Deepden Mound. Only the youngsters and some of the smaller females were there, Fara among them. They tried to find out from her what was happening.

'They have all gone to Rockhome, across the plain. I think they are going to…' she said vaguely, and then she wandered off.

They could discover no more. Sheena and Pebble left Sift to be looked after by Fara (when they found her again). The Utongo female was too afraid to go with them when they left the mound through the main entrance and set off for Rockhome: she did not want to be outside.

Sift had carried the dead pup, sadly, the remainder of the way to Deepden Mound. Pebble asked Fara to help her move it into the open air, and carry it to a place called High Level, which lay between two of the mounds off to the East. They would leave it there so that it would be found and taken by a bird of prey – an eagle or an owl, Sift hoped, rather than a vulture. Sheena thought Sift might well wait with the pup until that happened, and watch while it was carried off into the sky.

She was sorry about the pup's death, and sorry that she herself had been a part of it. She felt sorry for Sift, who had done her best. She felt sorry too for Slash, who had put his life in jeopardy to rescue his pup, but to no avail.

She felt even more concerned for him when she and Pebble reached Rockhome, having run as fast over the open ground as their tiredness would allow them.

Slash's life was very much at risk there. A Duwara sentry had seen the chase from The Gorge and across the plain, from his position half way up a lone tree between Deepden Mound and Rockhome. He had raced back to the Mound with the news. Tuft had hurriedly developed a plan, and Stab and Sandstepper had immediately been dispatched through the tunnels towards Rockhome. Tuft and Moon had gathered the rest of the tribe and set off in force, on the surface, to play their part in dealing with what they assumed was a new raid by the Utongo.

By the time Sheena and Pebble reached Rockhome, Stab and Sandstepper had already done what they needed to. They had persuaded Nungunungu to withdraw from the entrance to Rockhome, and instead block, further into the system, the tunnel leading from their den to Deepden Mound. They stayed there to make sure the porcupines did not turn again, in any sense of the word.

When they saw Nungu disappear further down the tunnel, Slash and his party had assumed he was retreating, and had entered Rockhome, thinking they would be able to find a way from there into the main system. Before long, however, they were confronted again, and halted, by Nungu's threatening spines. When they turned to leave, having decided they would need to seek another way into Deepden, they realised they were trapped. Tuft and the main party of Duwara had arrived outside. If the Utongo tried to escape through the narrow gap between the two rocks just outside the entrance, it could only be one by one, and one by one they would be killed.

That was the situation Sheena found when she and Pebble arrived. It was a situation she might not be able to do very much about. Tuft knew what an opportunity this was: a good part of the Utongo leadership could be destroyed here and now. That would make it much easier for the Duwara to rescue their three pups from Longburrow, and perhaps drive the Utongo out of The Gorge at the same time. Far from halting the wars, Sheena was beginning to think she had brought them to a new level.

The only good thing was that for the moment nothing much was likely to happen. Tuft was prepared to wait outside Rockhome. Nungu was content to leave his spiky rump blocking the tunnel, and have his face licked occasionally by Spickle. Slash would perhaps be expecting reinforcements from Longburrow.

Sheena did her best. Tuft, Moon and Crossclaw had climbed up on top of Rockhome to join the sentry who had been posted there. Sheena found her way up to them. She told them something of what had happened in Longburrow. She assured Tuft and Moon that their pups were being well treated. She explained that the Utongo thought the Duwara wanted to take over The Gorge for themselves, and perhaps even Longburrow.

She tried, in other words, to dispel some of the misunderstandings that divided the two tribes. She even attempted to say some good things about the Utongo.

That was where her Grand Plan went wrong again. Crossclaw in particular would hear nothing good about the enemies of the Duwara. The Utongo, or at least these Utongo, needed to be destroyed. They needed to be destroyed for what they were, and for what they had done, as much as for what they might do. That did not seem to be open for discussion. Sheena also suspected that in Crossclaw's view they should be destroyed because of what they believed. In Stab's absence Tuft was already planning ways of killing Slash and his group, some quite cruel ones among them.

Sheena's fears were being realised: the two tribes were in danger of turning this conflict into a war not of necessity but of revenge, a war about the past rather than the future. Such a war could lead only to a nasty, see-sawing balance between two roughly equal sides bent on wiping each other out…and it could last forever.

This would be a bad time to talk about the sun: she would have to wait for a much better opportunity to raise that subject.

In fact, she realised, she would have to *make* a much better opportunity. Part of the trouble was that she was not a meerkat: she was an outsider, listened to here only because she had done some helpful things for the Duwara. Even there, all was not well. Tuft thanked her for rescuing Pebble; but Moon angrily demanded to know why they had not brought her pups back with them.

Sheena could not explain that she had left them behind so that the Utongo would be able to use them to bargain with, especially now that she had failed to provide the Duwara with the Utongo equivalent – Slash's pup.

She needed to find a way of making sure the Duwara would pay attention to what she had to say, before she began to say it.

'Speak softly, and carry a big stick.'

Dad Allen had quoted that piece of advice at the family supper table, when the family had allowed him, once, to go on about international politics. It was about the art of Negotiation (rather than class control, Thomas was relieved to know).

Where could Sheena get a big stick from, though, something that would make both the Duwara and the Utongo step back from their warring and listen to her?

She soon knew.

Tuft and others were keeping a close eye on the line of trees that marked the beginning of The Gorge. Since she was facing them, Sheena was able to see in the opposite direction, off into the distance where the plains began to rise into low hills. Her attention was caught by a large, dark shape in the shade of a small group of trees some way off.

She looked harder, and was convinced. It was an elephant. She looked really hard, and was amazed once more. It was Mpole, Tembo Mpole, the Gradual Elephant.

Chapter Twenty-Five: Fimbo Kubwa

Wielded with care
Can do good rather than ill,
Will focus the mind
And teach goodwill.

She was riding back towards Rockhome on Mpole's head. He explained what he was doing here.

'I saw your family near their tents. You were not there. I followed the Land Rover tracks. They came in this direction and went back again. I thought I might find you near here. Then I heard some hrrummffaloes telling a strange story. I know you like to travel on animals' heads, so I guessed they must have been talking about you.'

Sheena had thought hrrummffaloes had short memories. It now seemed that their problem was only in concentrating on more than one thing at a time: they had remembered her, and she had passed into hrrummffalo lore.

She had travelled on Mpole's head when she had been helping him pass Mitihani Saba – the Seven Tests – a year earlier. She had also made two journeys (one of them a matter of life or death) sitting between a giraffe's blunt, furry horns. Now she was back where she had secretly, on each of those occasions, enjoyed being – in an elevated position on a large head, directing a large animal and large events.

She and Mpole had much to talk about, but now was not the time. She needed to explain what *she* was doing here, and why she so badly needed his help.

'I'm not sure what I'll want you to do…but just do it, please!' she said when she had finished explaining and they were nearing the pile of rocks. Mpole had benefitted greatly during their last time together from doing what she advised; she was sure he would now be willing take the risk of doing what she asked.

The situation at Rockhome had not changed at all during the short time Sheena had been away. Most of the Duwara were outside the entrance, patrolling up and down restlessly with regular forays off for food. Tuft, Moon and Crossclaw were still on top of the mound. Pebble had joined them, and had no doubt told them more about the events at Longburrow and in The Gorge.

They must all have been puzzled, a while ago, when Sheena suddenly scampered down from the rocks and set off across the plain. Now they would be even more mystified, as they watched her return in such a strange manner.

Sheena got Mpole to walk up the narrow path leading to the top of the mound until he reached the flat rock on which the four Duwara stood.

'I have an idea,' she said to them.

'Why don't you let Slash and the Utongo leave Rockhome? Then we can all get together out here and have a chat about what's going on. I think I may be able to help you sort out your little problems with each other.'

Sheena had a lot to learn about being a Negotiator. It was all very well to adopt an informal tone, and play down what was happening in order to reduce tension…so *get together* and *chat* were fine; but with *little problems* she had become condescending. That didn't work. Crossclaw reared up on his hind legs, ready to make a grand speech.

'There are no *little problems* here! Our borders have been violated! Our heritage is under threat! Our next generation has been taken hostage and is being held to ransom! Our sun has been insulted! We will soon see another sun appearing in the sky, if we are not careful.'

'Well, actually, er, that's what I wanted to talk to you about,' said Sheena, now that Crossclaw had given her an opening.

'I've just come back from Longburrow, and the sun there looks just the same as this one.'

She took a deep breath.

'I think there's only one sun.'

That was another mistake. Sheena had directly challenged one of the Duwara's basic beliefs and, perhaps even worse as far as negotiation was concerned, one of the foundations of Crossclaw's position within the tribe as the guardian of their faith. So she received a harsh rebuff from him.

'You silly patchwork creature, what do you know about it? Your very appearance gives you away! You have tried to be both black and white at the same time, and look at you! You are neither! You have nothing to hold you together! You need to return wherever you came from before you come apart at the seams and your bits of dry fur blow away on the wind.'

Mpole rumbled beneath her. She thought for a moment it might be with anger; then she was afraid it might be with laughter; but he was only passing a comment to her.

'I think you may have gone a bit too fast there,' he said.

She hoped the rumblings were too low for the meerkats to catch – she felt rather than heard what he was saying, through the vibrations of his skull.

Sheena had never had much hope of just talking the Duwara into anything, so she did not spend any more time trying. She had an alternative.

'Perhaps,' she said, as calmly as she could (*patchwork* had upset her a bit) 'you need a bit of time to think about what I've said…about letting the Utongo out, I mean.

'My friend Mpole and I will just go for a little stroll while you talk things over. Then we'll come back and see if you've changed your mind.'

She steered Mpole down from the hill, through the groups of other Duwara clustered at its foot, and away from Rockhome to the left of the line between there and Deepden Mound. There was another mound in that direction, not very far away. She remembered a fork in the tunnel not far from Rockhome, which probably led to it. She aimed Mpole towards a patch of bare ground under which she thought that branch of the tunnel might run.

Mpole wasn't at all fat as elephants go, but he was a taller, sturdier elephant than when she had last seen him. He also walked with a surer tread which she knew he would be able to turn into a heavier one if need be.

When they reached the bare patch she told Mpole to walk round in a circle. He did so without asking why. As they turned back towards Rockhome she could see that all the meerkats, on the hill and below it, were standing on their hind legs, watching closely.

'Now go round again,' she said. 'But stomp a bit this time.'

Mpole did as instructed. He put each foot down so solidly that the ground shook, and clouds of dust rose in the air.

Half-way round the second time he lurched forwards, suddenly. The earth had given way beneath one of his front feet.

The tunnel underneath had collapsed. He pulled his foot out of the hole he had made, and turned along what must be the line of the tunnel running below. He knew what Sheena was trying to do. Several times over the next few minutes his weight broke through the crust of earth above Deepden, exposing tunnels and chambers alike, all broken and looking rather pitiful now they were exposed to the air.

'Oh dear!' Sheena said as they arrived back at Rockhome and faced the four meerkats on the high stone slab.

'Sorry about your tunnel. Hope it wasn't an important one.

But you've got lots of others, haven't you?'

Crossclaw looked as if he had turned to stone himself. Only his eyes were alive, and they were fiery. Tuft and Moon, slightly behind him, stirred uncomfortably. Pebble seemed to be hiding at the back as if he did not want to become involved in this.

'Have you had a chance to think about my idea? Just let me know if you need more time. We can easily go for another stroll.'

Sheena had given Tuft and the Duwara a simple choice: either give up the idea of killing Slash and his party in order to defend Deepden, or lose it anyway, bit by bit, as Mpole criss-crossed the plain, making every ounce of his great weight felt.

She hoped it would not come to that; but there was no immediate response from the meerkats.

'Oh very well,' she said. 'We'll be back again shortly.

'I thought I might teach Mpole how to do your war dance, by the way. Would you mind? It *is* yours after all; but it's ever so impressive.'

When Slash and the other Utongo emerged from Rockhome they were suspicious. They knew how thoroughly trapped they had been. The Duwara meerkats stood on either side of the entrance, sullenly: they all felt that a great chance had not been taken; and they watched in silence as Slash led his small group out into the open air.

Sheena had spoken softly; and her big stick had done its job.

Chapter Twenty-Six: Kusafiri

*When you go on one
You can be lost without trace;
Or you may end where you began
But in a different place.*

Meerkats are great talkers, once they get going. The Duwara and the Utongo, however, had no intention of talking together. They talked at each other instead, and sometimes across each other, and over, past and under as well.

By now it was dusk. Slash had been allowed to bring his group up to the top of the mound, and settle with them on a flat rock almost at the same height as the one Tuft, Moon and Crossclaw were still occupying.

Stab and Sandstepper had joined the Duwara foursome. They had had to have some things explained to them.

Sheena had climbed onto another rock, between the two but at a slightly lower level. She had foolishly thought she might be able to do some more Negotiating, this time between the two groups rather than just with one of them. Instead she found herself witnessing a lot of jumping, and hissing, and growling, with some additional stamping amid clouds of dust. What she heard, in addition, was lots of blame, much history, some very empty statements ('The sun is the sun!') and several nasty threats.

She had decided that to begin with both tribes should be

Kusafiri

allowed to say what they felt; what they clearly felt like *doing* however was leaping over her to tear out each others' throats.

The few Utongo were at a disadvantage. Down below on the flat ground the rest of the Duwara were still gathered, listening carefully to what was being said above, and every now and again there was angry muttering among them. Twice it looked as if they were on the point of surging up among the rocks to attack Slash and his companions. On each occasion Sheena had to signal to Mpole to walk a little way in the direction of Deepden Mound. That had the effect of calming the situation down immediately.

A difficult moment occurred when Slash demanded that the Duwara return his pup. It fell to Tuft to reply. He did so bluntly.

'Your pup is dead. We did not kill it. It must have been a weakling.'

There was much muttering among the Utongo. Slash himself said nothing, but Sheena thought she saw his long claws twitch. Surely he was not thinking of attacking the whole Duwara tribe, with so few companions alongside him?

Eventually both sides seemed to have run out of accusations, distortions, extremisms and warnings. Sheena decided now was the time for her to speak.

'I have another idea,' she said.

Just then, however, things began to go badly wrong again. There was a cry from some of the Duwara below.

'The Utongo! The Utongo are here!'

The bushes along the nearest stretch of The Gorge shook at ground level, and what must have been nearly the whole of the Utongo tribe appeared, almost simultaneously. Once they were in the open they stood upright, paused, then dropped onto all fours again and began to stream over the plain towards Rockhome, gradually converging.

The Duwara down on the plain turned to face them, and started their hissing and their growling and their war-dance, little effect though any of that was likely to have.

Sheena needed to do something; but what?

Mpole now showed some of the quickness he had acquired during Mitihani Saba. As soon as he saw what was happening he leant his great weight forward and set off to meet the Utongo. He did not hurry, however. In fact, he soon stopped, and began kicking at the ground, causing quantities of dust to drift up into the air.

'Surely that's not his attempt at a war-dance,' Sheena thought. 'It's not very convincing. It's a pity I didn't get to teach him how to do it properly.'

It was all rather casual, in fact. All Mpole was doing was make a pile of loose sand. The Utongo would be able to run round it, and him, all too easily.

They came closer to where he stood. He stuck the end of his trunk into the pile. As the meerkats approached, dividing so that they could run past him on either side, he lifted his trunk and sprayed them forcefully with a mixture of sand and pebbles. The blasts were powerful enough to knock the meerkats at the front of the two columns off their feet and bowl them over backwards.

Sheena had seen elephants suck in dust and blow it over their bodies as a protection against heat and insects, but that was quite a gentle process, almost as if they were puffing talcum powder under their armpits; by comparison what Mpole was doing was like firing a blunderbuss, an old-fashioned, wide-muzzled shotgun, at the advancing meerkats.

He re-loaded his trunk several times, and every time the Utongo got to their feet and tried to come forward he blew them down and back again. They soon stopped. They broke into

211

muttering, dusty groups watching and listening from a distance.

'As I was saying,' Sheena continued calmly (Mpole had stayed where he was, separating the two tribes). 'I have another idea.

'Why don't we see whether there really are two suns?'

'How can we do that?' said Crossclaw scornfully. 'This is not about seeing. We stop *seeing* as soon as we enter The Gorge. We know our sun stays over Deepden when we leave, otherwise those of us who remain here would find ourselves in darkness. So our sun does not travel with us. The sun we have seen on the other side of The Gorge must therefore be a different one. It is the Utongo sun – for what that is worth.'

'It is worth a great deal!'

Slash had broken in, angrily.

'It is worth fifty of your Duwara suns. You can have as many of those as you wish. They are illusions. That one up there now…' he nodded upwards, but without looking up himself, '…is no more than a poor copy.'

Crossclaw ignored him and carried on addressing Sheena.

'If you do not accept my reasoning, it does not matter. This is a matter of faith, not proof.'

It was very difficult to argue against any of that, particularly the faith part. The chameleon had said something about that, hadn't it? If a mere lizard could persuade itself it was a leaf, and then become a leaf, a meerkat could perhaps convince itself of anything.

Sheena did not plan to argue, however, but to show.

'Your sun does not go with you when you travel through The Gorge, you say. Has a meerkat ever travelled *around* The Gorge?'

'Ha! Around The Gorge? The Gorge is very long. Why would any meerkat travel around it when he can go through it, and eat well on the way? There is nothing at either of its ends any different from what we have here.'

'Yes there is,' said Sheena. 'A chance to look round the corner.'

Slash now spoke again, a little more thoughtfully than Crossclaw had done.

'I have heard that a Utongo meerkat once made that journey – around the end of The Gorge from Longburrow and back again. When he returned, however, he could talk only madness, and he soon died.

'None of us has gone that way since. There is no need, and there is great danger.'

'There *is* a need,' said Sheena. 'And there will be great danger if you do *not* make the journey. You are very close to destroying one another, just because each of you believes your own tribe is better since it lives under a better sun.

'If you knew that you were living under the *same* sun, maybe that belief would change. Maybe you would begin to see that the things you have in common are much more important than the things that make you different. Maybe you'd do more sharing and less shouting. Maybe you would learn to live for the future rather than in the past.'

That was much more of a speech than Sheena had intended to make: she had got carried away, and ended up impressing herself. She seemed to have impressed Mpole too. He trumpeted loudly, startling everybody, as if to say, 'Way to go, little cat!' He followed that up by a few steps out towards Deepden Mound and back again, and then with a snort of sand and pebbles towards the Utongo meerkats still grouped some distance from Rockhome. All the meerkats were very well behaved.

It was difficult to tell whether it was Sheena's words or Mpole's reminders that had proved more persuasive. Sheena had her own views on that. Whichever was the case, she felt very satisfied as she set off next morning, towards the point where the line of The Gorge met the horizon. Tuft and Slash were with her. Mpole had stayed behind to keep the peace.

Chapter Twenty-Seven: Duma

We are not leopard
But have spots all the same,
And we're honest hunters
Despite our name.

They had not known whether they should head right or left along The Gorge: there was no tribal memory among the meerkats to tell them which end was nearer.

They turned right. Slash soon complained.

'I cannot travel so far with the Duwara sun in my eyes.'

Sheena pointed out that well before they reached the end of The Gorge the sun would probably be at their backs.

'Would you rather have it in your eyes near the end of our journey, when you are tired?'

It had been a long and difficult night. As the sun disappeared, all the meerkats had settled down where they were, to make the best of things. The Utongo had no wish to attempt the journey back through The Gorge in darkness; and the Duwara would not have felt safe within Deepden, knowing that large numbers of Utongo were on the plain outside.

They all looked after themselves as best they could: by the time night fell there were piles of meerkats surrounding Rockhome. Everyone wanted a warm spot near the bottom of his or her pile, and much wriggling, tottering and tumbling took place before things were stable, and quiet.

The meerkats became very cold as the night wore on. Sheena, sleeping alone, suffered almost as much, even with her thicker coat. Only Mpole slept well.

Dawn, when it came, had been very interesting. The Duwara woke quickly, obviously in need of much warming from their sun. Tuft, Moon, Crossclaw and Pebble, who had stayed on their rock platform, stood up proudly and let the sunlight brighten their eyes and their fur. Many of the other Duwara climbed up onto Rockhome's lower levels to enjoy Sunwake.

The main body of Utongo, a little way out on the plain, stood too, in their many small groups; but as the sun showed above the horizon they turned away from it. Sheena wondered whether this was a show of rejection: perhaps the Utongo were declaring that they wanted nothing to do with this Other Sun. Perhaps, however, like Sift, they had simply found it painful, even frightening, to look at.

Then it occurred to her that they might be desperately hoping to see their own sun rise on the other side of The Gorge, away to the left where the line of trees disappeared in the distance.

It did not; and whether they felt any of this sun's warmth, and whether they were at all grateful for it, Sheena could not tell.

The rock on which Slash and his companions had spent the night was between the rising sun and Tuft's platform. When the sun came up, these Utongo also rose to their full height and turned their backs on the bright white disc. Was it by chance that the shadows they cast fell on the Duwara leaders so that they had to move to one side to receive the full benefit of the warming rays? Sheena could not tell that, either.

Neither Slash nor Tuft was willing to allow the other to be in front as they travelled along the edge of The Gorge – Tuft because as far as he was concerned this was still Deepden, his Deepden, Slash because they were heading towards Longburrow, *his* home territory. Sheena had to take the lead to prevent some undignified jostling.

The two meerkat leaders did not want to be here at all, it was plain, following in the footsteps of this disrespectful and coercive cat creature on a pointless mission to prove what was unproveable because it was not true.

Sheena tried to keep some sort of conversation going with the two meerkats behind her, afraid that they would suddenly leap at each other, without a Mpole to get in the way – or a Mum Allen, skilful in the art of keeping angry children apart.

She wondered briefly where her family were right now. Still back at the campsite, she hoped, still back at the campsite for another few days so that she would be able to do all she could for the meerkats (which might in the end be nothing) and get back there herself in time to sneak aboard *Great White* before it roared off towards home.

'Oh, I wanted to ask you, Slash – how did you get on with Mondo? You were three-nil down when we had to leave. What was the final score?'

'The final score was one-nil to us,' said Slash grimly. 'It was *very* final.'

That could mean only one thing. So much for Mondo's pride in her fighting prowess.

So much, too, for Sheena's first attempt at chit-chat: Slash clearly had nothing more to say on the matter. She tried Tuft.

'I've wondered, Tuft: where did Moon get her name?'

'She's called Moon because she's very changeable.'

There was grimness in Tuft's response, also, but it was a mock grimness that was almost humour. This reply was as short and unhelpful as Slash's had been, however, and Sheena had to struggle to keep the conversation going.

'How many moons do you think there are, by the way?'

That was as good a next question to ask as any: she would perhaps learn something more about how meerkat minds worked.

'There are as many moons as there have been nights since the world began. Have you not seen? Every moon is different.'

Perhaps meerkat memories only lasted a month. Sheena did not argue the point. Arguing with meerkats, she had found, was like wriggling your way through heavy floor-length curtains when you wanted to get out into the garden sunshine, then finding a solid, locked door behind them.

It was Tuft who had answered her, but then Slash also spoke.

'That is why we believe in the sun, not the moon. The sun does not change. It is always there for us, and it is always complete.'

The Duwara and the Utongo were in agreement about one thing, then.

'What happens when the sun can't be seen – when it's cloudy?'

'We talk about it to remind ourselves of what it looks like.'

'We talk about it a great deal; but we are always amazed when we see it again. It is always more beautiful, and more powerful, than we remembered it.'

Slash had taken up where Tuft left off. They could have been talking about the same sun; but then they were, as far as Sheena was concerned...

Sheena returned to the subject again, a little later, when they had travelled a good distance along the edge of The Gorge and were well out of sight of Rockhome.

'Do other meerkat tribes, in other parts of Baragandiri, have their own suns?'

'Yes, but they too are false,' said Tuft.

'Like the Utongo sun.'

'Like the Duwara sun,' said Slash at the same time.

Their utter faith in the supremacy of their own sun was remarkable. Was there no place in a meerkat mind where doubt could live? It would all have been easier to explain if the meerkats had *had* two brains. One brain could then have believed in the sun all it liked, and the other one would have been free to believe what it wanted to.

It was early afternoon. The sun had passed overhead and now shone hotly down from a little way behind. They had had to stop more and more often to grub at the edge of the vegetation for something moistureful to eat.

They had no way of telling how far it might be to the end of The Gorge. At no great distance the trees and bushes dwindled into a shaky line that then disappeared in the heat haze.

In fact, Sheena realised with something of a shock, it had perhaps been a mistake to assume that The Gorge *had* an end.

Didn't all things have an end, however?

She was just beginning to wonder whether The Gorge went round in a vast circle, when the vegetation began to thin out, and it became apparent that the valley had become quite shallow. They could see the rise of its other side through the trees closest to them.

Sheena was relieved. Then the cheetahs arrived.

There were three of them, and they came walking smoothly over the plain. At least the mother, who was in front, came walking smoothly. The two youngsters behind her came bounding, in stops and starts, then every now and again in something approaching a smooth walk when they remembered that was what they were supposed to be doing.

They were heading straight for the three travellers. The female cheetah had obviously noticed them. She moved very purposefully, but also gracefully, her high shoulders hunching and rolling every time she put a front paw to the ground. She was built very like Mondo, with a long body and small head, but did not look quite so stretched. She was also much bigger. Her sleek coat had a very even spread of black spots.

The two youngsters were trouble size.

Ordinarily the cheetahs would not have posed much of a threat to the meerkats, who would just have dived into the line of bushes alongside which they were travelling, and hidden until the danger had passed. The cheetahs, great runners and hunters on the open plain, would not have followed them into such dense vegetation.

Tuft and Slash moved to do just that. Sheena quickly jumped between them and the greenery.

'No!' she cried. 'If we all go into the bushes we will lose sight of the sun. We are very near the end of The Gorge. When we come out again how will we know it is the same sun shining on us?'

She was very anxious that neither of the meerkats should have any excuse for denying what she was bent on showing them – the sun's one-ness.

'There must always be one of us out here. I'll stay first.'

So there began a very strange game of hide-and-streak.

The female cheetah wanted her cubs to have some hunting practice. They for their part were happy to chase anything that ran away from them. So when the two meerkats now made a dash for the cover of the bushes the cubs raced after them, ignoring Sheena, who had stayed very still. When they were past her she strolled off nonchalantly, still parallel with The Gorge, leaving all three cheetahs behind. The adult cheetah showed no interest in her either, as she walked off. The cheetah family did not seem to be in need of food, for the moment: the female was there only to supervise the youngsters' training.

Tuft and Slash had understood what was needed. Once they were safely into the bushes, they turned and raced along among them, following a line a little way in from the plain. Sheena heard the rustling of their passage as they went by her, but could not see them; and they were soon well ahead of her.

The cubs, once the meerkats had vanished, slowed to a walk. Then they turned their attention towards Sheena, and began to pad after her as she walked steadily away from them. She knew that if she broke into a run they would break into a dash and be on her in no time. Her other instinct was to dive into the bushes herself; but she could not do that until one of the meerkats reappeared to take over from her the responsibility of ensuring that nothing happened to the sun.

The cubs were soon much too close for comfort.

'Hello-o! Is anybody there?' she called forward.

Some way ahead the bushes parted and Tuft leapt out into the open. He looked back briefly, saw how close the cubs were to Sheena, and began running away, but not at full speed. The cubs immediately bunched their hind legs and sprang forward past Sheena.

It was her turn to take refuge among the vegetation, but as she ran forward through it she kept popping her head out to see what was happening ahead.

The cheetahs accelerated alarmingly: she could hardly believe how quickly they were catching up with Tuft. It looked as if he would have to jump back into the bushes immediately, to escape them. She would need to be ready to leap out into the open again, otherwise the sun would be out of sight of all of them, and the whole enterprise would be in jeopardy.

Then, just in time, Slash appeared, further ahead along the edge of The Gorge. He stood still, brown against the green, looking back to check on the sun. As soon as Tuft saw him he himself swerved into the vegetation and disappeared. That brought the cubs to a temporary halt. There was nothing running, so there was nothing to chase.

They soon began to trot onwards, however, towards Slash, the only animal they could now see. He remembered to walk on, slowly, rather than run. That would give Tuft some time to get ahead of him, ready to take over the next leg of the relay.

Sheena in the meanwhile continued to move forward through the bushes as quickly as she could.

All too soon, however, the cubs were close enough to Slash to force him into a run. They then sprang forward after him, travelling at several times his speed. In a moment they would take him. There was no sign of Tuft.

Then suddenly Tuft was there again, out of the bushes and even further along the edge of the plain…but not far enough, nor still enough. Slash saw him and shot into the undergrowth. This time the cubs hardly broke stride: they continued to race on, and would very quickly get to where Tuft was, before Slash had a chance to run beyond him through the greenery.

This was not going to work. The cubs were too fast. The vegetation was too difficult to run through. Sheena had to draw the cubs back, away from the meerkats.

She broke free of the vegetation and ran out onto the plain, at right angles to The Gorge. That was a very risky thing to do; but she needed Tuft to know that she was out there, able to see the sun, so that he could jump straight back into the bushes without attempting to lead the cheetahs further on: they were much too close for that.

He saw her, and turned and dashed quickly into the cover. The cubs, at a loss once more, looked round and noticed Sheena out on the plain, well away from the safety of The Gorge. They instantly turned and set off towards her at a trot. Slash and Tuft would be able to make good progress along the edge of the vegetation before either of them needed to come out into the open again.

Sheena hoped she had not badly misjudged things. She turned back towards The Gorge, still running. She could not risk slowing to a walk: if the cubs got close to her before she was near the line of bushes, she was lost.

The cubs increased their pace, chasing towards her from the side, trying to cut her off. She had certainly bought time for Slash and Tuft...but would she as certainly survive?

It would be a very close thing. The young cheetahs were flying along towards her, their heads maintaining a steady and frightening line, their paws hardly touching the ground.

Sheena's much smaller paws were slipping in the sandy earth, slowing her down. She would not make it, she would not make it, the cubs were nearly between her and the bushes and she had to veer away from her straight line, hoping to get past them at an angle.

Then, horrified, she realised the mother cheetah was running up behind her and slightly to her left. She would be caught between parent and offspring, knocked over, gripped by the throat with sharp teeth, and have her air supply cut off so that she slowly suffocated. That was how cheetahs killed their prey.

Sheena's life did not flash before her eyes, but the reason why she was about to die ran through her mind. Slash and Tuft were now probably far enough away to be able to escape, finally. If she was killed, would they carry on with their quest? Very unlikely, since they did not believe in it. What a waste it would all have been!

The female cheetah overtook her and slewed round to a halt in front of her. Sheena prepared herself.

'Stop!'

The cheetah's voice was one to be obeyed. Sheena stopped.

The order had been given not to her, however, but to the cubs. They too came to a sudden halt, very close to Sheena. Too close. They were panting. Would they soon start drooling?

'You need not kill this creature; but you need to learn from it.

'Do not always chase the running animal. The animal that walks can be just as tasty.'

Then she turned to Sheena. Sheena decided her face was rather gentle, now that it was not racing up behind her with its teeth bared. Thin black markings ran down from her eyes to the corners of her mouth, like two lines of tears, and that gave her a sorrowful look, as if life were difficult for her.

'Thank you,' said the cheetah. 'That was a useful lesson. You are training your offspring well. If other animals learnt to work together like that in order to escape, our hunting would become much more difficult.

'Only one in ten of our chases ends in a kill as it is.'

'They are not my offspring,' Sheena felt she had to say. 'They are not even the same kind of animal.'

'All the more remarkable, then, and all the more worrying.

'You can all go on your way; but I'd rather you did not teach any other animals how to co-operate.'

Sheena had left by the time the cheetah finished her sentence…but she was careful not to run.

Chapter Twenty-Eight: Pembe

When you turn me
You will face in a different direction,
And if you choose to walk on
You may make a new connection.

They had to take Sheena's word for it, both the meerkats, that on the one occasion they had both been under the cover of the trees at the same time, nothing had happened to the sun. The fact that they were prepared to believe her was a sign that they were also beginning to trust her. So they should: she had just risked her life in this whole business, hadn't she?

However, 'We do not expect the sun to change until we are right at the end of The Gorge,' Tuft said, which spoilt things a bit.

'That is when we will cross the line between Duwara territory and Utongo.'

Did Sheena detect a note of defiance in Tuft's voice, indicating a touch of uncertainty? She hoped so: that in itself would be something of a breakthrough. Faith could be good; but doubt was sometimes better. Perhaps there *was* a place in the meerkat mind for questions rather than just answers.

They had stopped to rest, and eat, soon after their encounter with the cheetahs; but they could not stay long. They needed to reach the end of The Gorge before nightfall and get well round it.

Sheena knew that if they were only close to it by the time the sun went down, when it came up again next morning there would be a squabble over whose sun it was.

They quickened their pace. Soon they could see a tree that seemed to be the last of the line, surrounded by low bushes and standing singly against the sky.

All three of them kept a careful eye on the sun, pausing frequently to look at it as they approached what would be a turning point in their journey. It was more than three-quarters of the way down the sky. Soon they would round the corner and be on Utongo ground; then they might just be able to see Longburrow; at that moment, Sheena hoped, she would be able to ask the two meerkats to look at the sun together and admit that it was the same one they had begun their journey under.

Quite what would happen after that she did not know. What was about to take place was a shaking of the foundations for both tribes, and there was no telling how their leaders would react. She did not expect Slash and Tuft, however, to fall on each other's shoulders and weep tears of reconciliation.

They eventually reached the tree.

'What are *they*?' Slash asked. He had been looking directly away from the soon-to-be-setting sun, following the line The Gorge would have taken if it had not stopped right here, where they were. The things he had noticed were in an area of the Park so far from both Longburrow and Deepden that neither the Utongo nor the Duwara would have much interest in claiming it as theirs.

Sheena knew the answer.

'They're tents,' she said.

'Humans sleep in them when they are away from their houses.'

These were not like the tents of a campsite, however, which were usually of different shapes, sizes and colours and set up in higgledy-piggledy fashion. They were all white, the same size and shape, and standing in a neat row. There was no sign of movement around them.

Both meerkats were uneasy at the thought of humans so near The Gorge.

'I think we should go and investigate,' said Slash.

'Yes,' Tuft agreed.

Sheena knew this was just another way of putting off the moment when the meerkats might have to face a new reality. The sun was close to the horizon. There was no time to lose.

'No! We must hurry towards Longburrow!' Sheena said.

She turned away from the tents and back towards the setting sun. She was not at all sure Slash and Tuft would follow her, but did not dare look over her shoulder in case that might reveal her uncertainty.

She rounded a clump of bushes, further into what was undoubtedly Utongo territory. There, in the very far distance ahead of them, and almost out of sight, she could see the first of the line of mounds that was Longburrow, with the low sun behind it. Now she had to risk a look backwards.

She was relieved to see Slash and Tuft close behind. They soon caught up. All three of them stopped to look at the sun. It was now just touching the hard line of the plains.

'So, my good meerkat friends. Which sun is that?'

'The Duwara sun,' said Tuft.

'The Utongo sun,' said Slash.

'But is it the same sun?' Sheena asked.

There was a long pause. Everything depended on this moment. Sheena looked from one meerkat to the other, wondering which would reply first. In the end they spoke at the same time.

'Yes, it is the same sun,' they both replied.

Chapter Twenty-Nine: Mjengaji

We devour land
Fill empty spaces
Spoil the unspoilt
And destroy special places.

They had to travel through much of the night to reach the nearest Longburrow mound. There was no meerkat on sentry duty there, and Slash felt no need to make their presence known. He had a lot of thinking to do before he faced any of the other Utongo, most of whom in any case were still back at Rockhome. Both he and Tuft had been silent for the remainder of the journey, and Sheena had decided not to be cheery.

They slept briefly in the tunnels beneath the mound, and just before dawn climbed up onto it. The sun when it rose sent its light flooding over the plain. Slash stood facing it, gathering new strength. Tuft was slower to rise onto his hind legs and open himself to it; but when he did it was clear that he was taking from it what he needed – not just warmth, but confirmation that what had happened the day before was real. He knew he was looking at a sun that was both Duwara and Utongo.

In the distance they could see, standing on top of one of the central mounds, the few Utongo meerkats who had remained when the rest of the tribe left for Deepden. They were mainly youngsters, together with four or five females. Slash decided he needed to reassure them that all was well, before they set off to return to Deepden through The Gorge: they would no doubt have been seen.

'Don't you want to go back the way we came, to do a double check on the single sun?' Sheena had asked, hoping very much that that they would not.

'Or maybe you want to go all the way round the other end of The Gorge, to make sure nothing strange happens there when you cross back into Duwara territory?'

Perhaps there was no other end of The Gorge (but didn't something with one end have to have another one?) In any case she felt it very unlikely that the meerkats, after what they had been through, would want to follow her suggestion.

'No. We have seen. Now we must tell.'

Tuft seemed to be speaking for both meerkats. Through The Gorge it would be, then, once they had visited the Utongo on the distant mound.

They were barely half-way there when they heard the distant roar of engines.

There were no vehicles in sight. The roar got slowly louder. The group of Utongo on the mound had turned in alarm towards the sound, which was coming from behind a line of trees well away from The Gorge, behind and to the right of where Sheena and the others had just stopped.

A Land Rover emerged from behind the trees, and two pick-up trucks, then another Land Rover. It was possible that they had come from the line of tents out on the plains.

The early sunlight glinted on their windscreens. Neither of the Land Rovers was white.

The column of vehicles was driving slowly. They were not following a track. There was no track. They were heading straight for the centre of Longburrow, where the other meerkats were. They were still a long way away from both the main Longburrow mound and the point where Sheena, Slash and Tuft had halted.

'We must get to Heartmound quickly,' said Slash. 'The tunnels are in danger.'

The three of them began to run. Once more Sheena found herself in a race.

They won this one. They reached the mound when the vehicles were only half-way from the trees: the Land Rovers and pick-ups had slowed down further as the ground became bumpier, and were now bouncing along jerkily; but they were still travelling straight towards the Longburrow system.

Slash was first to get to the meerkat group on the mound. They had not moved from their upright posture, faces pointed forward intently at the oncoming vehicles as if they were onlookers at the scene of an imminent traffic accident. The only traffic accident, however, would happen to them, if they did not move.

'Quick! We must clear the tunnels!' Slash cried.

'But they're empty,' one of the females replied. 'The Ndugu have taken our injured to Gorgeden, so that they are nearer the Healing Groves. Only the Duwara pups are in the Heartmound tunnels, now'

'They aren't empty then!' said Slash sharply; and he led the way into the main tunnel entrance. Tuft followed him. Tuft followed him to help rescue the Duwara pups, which were his pups, and Moon's, and part of the Duwara future – a different Duwara future now, whether they liked it or not.

Several of the females went as well. Sheena did not. She wanted to watch what was happening above ground. By the time Slash and the others appeared again, three of the females with very small pups dangling from their mouths, she had seen something very interesting.

'We must take shelter in the trees! Head for The Gorge!' Slash cried; and he led the way.

Sheena stayed. She had nothing much to fear from the vehicles or the people in them, and she wanted to know why they were here.

She soon found out. They were here to examine this part of the Park. They were here to measure distances and angles and levels and depths, and take soil samples (but not plant samples). They were here to draw up plans, of a very different kind from any of Sheena's.

Sheena had seen people like this in action before, on the Caribbean island she came from. They were Developers. (Dad Allen had once called them Develepers, as if they carried a terrible disease that could threaten whole communities. He knew a lot about the sickness, since he had often helped out, along with some of his students, at a local Leprosy Trust village.) They would be here, no doubt, to decide whether or not this was a good location for a Safari Lodge, so that people could sit in armchairs and drink coffee while they watched elephants as if they were just seeing them on television.

Sheena had withdrawn to a tree nearer The Gorge, and climbed it. From there she had a clear view of the vehicles and what they were doing.

They drove straight over what must be the main Longburrow tunnel linking the mounds. Then they turned and drove back again. Then they drove up and down, almost half the length of Longburrow. Sheena could see from where she stood that they were doing a lot of damage. Time after time a wheel would sink into the ground as the tunnel beneath collapsed, then an engine

233

would rev and wheels would spin and sand would fly, and another tunnel or another chamber would be destroyed. It was almost as if the drivers were doing it deliberately. Slash would be able to see it happening too, from the safety of the bushes at the edge of The Gorge, and he would be enraged, helplessly enraged.

Eventually the vehicles stopped. Men got out, unloaded lots of equipment (what looked like small telescopes on legs; long poles marked off in red and white segments; large tape measures; big drills for making test holes in the ground; a satellite dish; clipboards; laptop computers and small tables on which to place them) and set about checking whether or not this would be a good place to build. Sheena decided she would help them make up their minds.

The interesting thing she had seen while Slash and Tuft were underground, the interesting thing she had seen in the far distance, well North of the Gorge, was what looked from here like Sungusungu, innumerable black ants spread across the landscape and moving slowly, en masse, in this direction. They were so far away, however, that they had to be not insects but large animals.

She had wondered...and looked harder...and was soon certain. They *were* Mbogo – hrrummffaloes – but many more than had been in the group that had nearly destroyed Deepden. Were those same animals among this larger herd?

She needed to get to them as quickly as possible. So she ran, then ran some more, then did some running, then rested and ran again. All the time the herd of hrrummffaloes got closer and closer. Luckily, they were coming towards her ...but not fast enough, not nearly fast enough, she feared.

It turned out, however, that she had plenty of time. After a while the men got back into their vehicles and drove a little further along the plain, keeping the same distance from The Gorge. They worked some more, then they stopped for a break, unloading cool boxes containing food and drink and setting up folding chairs nearby.

Sheena saw all of that by halting every now and again to look back. Before long she was very near the hrrummffaloes. She was seeking out one in particular – the great dense brute she had learned to steer, the leader of the first group and perhaps the leader also of this herd.

When she had talked with the Duwara about that encounter at Deepden, she had given him the name Big Hrumph. He was there, towards the front, snuffling heavily along, stopping every now and again to crop a clump of the sparse grass. The two white birds were not sitting on his head, but one was perched on his rump; and he was still drooling slobber.

She wove and dodged her way through the forest of black legs belonging to the nearer hrrummffaloes. The massive animals moved away from her, uneasily, as if some of them at least remembered her. She came close to Big Hrumph, and waited for him to lower his head to feed once more. Then she leapt up on top of his curved horns and dug her claws into the hairy skin covering his bony head, just as she had the first time.

The legend of the black-and-white flying creature came horribly alive once more, for Big Hrumph. If hrrummffaloes could have headaches this was one, and it was back again, pulling at his skull with sharp hooks even more painfully than last time. Then it jumped down to where it could dig its claws into his nose. He set off to chase it, ram it, toss it, trample it; and Sheena steered him the way she wanted to go.

By the time the thundering herd came close to the men, they had started their digging, drilling, measuring and calculating again. They soon stopped.

You can easily tell the next part of the story yourself, if not on paper then in your head. You know Sheena well enough by now; and you'll have guessed what her plan was…

At the end, when the men have escaped in what may be the only driveable vehicle, you may want to explain how Sheena relieved Big Hrumph's headache and joined the meerkats at the edge of The Gorge, and how Mbogo gradually became Sungusungu once more.

Chapter Thirty: Kufa

I smell most sweet
And smile on each guest.
All who come to me
Eternally rest.

It had been a great victory, a failed defence and a delayed defeat all in one. The men had been routed, but Longburrow had been largely destroyed; and the men would no doubt return.

Nature, under attack, had fought back through the hrrummffaloes (with a little help from a cat); but it would take stronger forces to stem the advance of mankind into the wilderness. Maybe in the darkness of The Gorge, Sheena thought, there was something that would turn the tide. In the meanwhile all she could do was help the meerkats towards a new life.

It made sense for the small group of Utongo females and youngsters to accompany Slash and Tuft and Sheena back through The Gorge, by the easiest route. There was nothing much here for them now.

That solved one problem Sheena thought she was going to have – how to help Tuft get his three pups back to Deepden. The Utongo females carried them, taking turns.

Some of the females were anxious about leaving the Utongo sun behind. They had not been into The Gorge before.

'Don't worry,' Slash reassured them. 'Our own sun will be waiting for us on the far side.'

'How can that be?' one female asked.

He did not answer. He had not worked out yet how to explain what he now knew.

Tuft, for his part, would no doubt be turning over in his mind what he would say to the Duwara, and in particular to Crossclaw. If he failed to find the right words, it might be necessary for the whole tribe to make the journey he had just made…

The Utongo youngsters frisked around the group as they set off, and were excited to be among the trees, but they soon quietened down when the sides of The Gorge became steeper and the vegetation thicker, and they all had to walk carefully.

It was just as gloomy in the Gorge as when Sheena had been here on the two previous occasions. She listened carefully for the tramp of tiny marching feet and a rustling in the undergrowth, but they reached the dry stream bed without incident. Several times on this first part of the journey Slash and Tuft had walked alongside one another, talking quietly.

Climbing the other side of the valley they passed close to the piece of level ground where Mondo had made her stand, and Sheena glimpsed four long, elegant legs sticking up stiffly in the air from a patch of tall grass. Mondo was lying on her back; and she was lifeless. Her polished claws glinted in the gloom, but several of them were broken and hanging at strange angles. There was a trace of perfume in the air, but also another, even sweeter smell. Sheena said nothing to Slash, and he said nothing to her.

Well into the day, and just before the trees began to thin out towards the Duwara edge of The Gorge, Sheena noticed a thick tree-branch watching them with a single, rotating eye. No-one else saw it.

Chapter Thirty-One: Jumla

I sound empty
But really I'm not.
Put two halves together
And I'm what you've got.

'We have nothing to say tonight. We will talk to you tomorrow.'

It was Tuft who spoke; but Slash was alongside him on the rock platform.

In their absence the area around Rockhome had remained in a state of high tension, with both tribes facing each other belligerently. The Utongo occupied most of the plain nearby, and the Duwara held their position outside the tunnel entrance. The meerkats from both tribes had left and returned in small groups, going off regularly to forage and then coming back to Rockhome because they did not know what else to do.

Word of why Slash and Tuft had set off with Sheena towards Longburrow had spread quickly through both sides. Very few of the meerkats made any comment: the suggestion that there might be only one sun was so strange to them that they could find nothing to say.

Moon was silent most of the time, lying on a rock half-way up Rockhome and standing every now and again to peer towards the end of The Gorge Tuft had left for, as if she expected him to return from there. Stab spent his time moving round among the Duwara, preparing them for battle in case events turned in that direction. Crossclaw had disappeared into the main tunnel system as soon as Tuft left, and had not been seen since.

The Utongo were clearly uneasy in their exposed position. Tassel and Streak seemed to have the task of holding the tribe together and keeping up their spirits, which they did by chirruping their way around the groups and doing some licking of fur.

Mpole had found some shade. He did not sleep, however.

Now, towards the end of this long day, with both meerkat leaders back at Rockhome, the Duwara and the Utongo alike were hoping for an account of what had happened.

Some of them, however, would have been satisfied by a re-statement of old, loud things that they would find comforting even if it led them back to the brink of battle.

They all had to wait until the next morning.

Not a single meerkat was asleep when the sky began to lighten. The deep indigo of the night slowly turned to a mid-blue, and a pale yellow line crept along the flat horizon. Then the top curve of the sun appeared, and the first flood of glorious light began to pour smoothly across the plain towards Rockhome, turning what had been grey to gold.

Slash and Tuft were standing on the highest point of Rockhome, side by side, their faces towards the coming dawn. They were alone.

Moon was on her flat rock at a lower level, with her three pups. The pups had spent the night in one of the Rockhome chambers, but as morning approached they had been carried carefully out into the cold air and laid gently on the hard surface.

Their heads moved restlessly, as if they thought it was about time they were fed again, and they gave an occasional gentle squeak. There was still no sign of Crossclaw.

The other meerkats were looking in one of three directions. Some of the Duwara faced the sun as it rose. Some of the Utongo very deliberately had their backs to it. Most of the meerkats, however, from both tribes, were watching Tuft and Slash.

Sheena, on top of Mpole's head, was watching everyone.

The sunlight reached the two leaders first, in their elevated position. Its golden brightness touched the tops of their heads and settled slowly over their bodies so that the darkness cloaking their fur was washed downwards into the cracks among the rocks, intensifying the darkness already there. Both meerkats, revealed, glowed against the pale morning sky.

'This is both Sunwatch and Sunwake,' said Tuft, so that all could hear.

'We have given it a new name. It is called Sunshare.'

Slash spoke also. 'The sun that we now see is both the Utongo sun and the Duwara sun. It is the Meerkat sun. It is the Only Sun; and it is even greater than we knew.'

Sheena would have been pleased, now, to witness a great shifting, of both feet and minds, as all the meerkats turned and faced the old sun and acknowledged this new truth. This was life, however, not a story, and that did not happen. There was no sudden coming together. What there was instead was hubbub and confusion, with meerkats milling around left, right and in the middle, and a general dustiness rising into the air.

Tuft and Slash came down from the top of Rockhome and moved around among the scattered and anxious groups.

The sunlight continued to move over the plain, and before

241

long all the meerkats were bathed in its strengthening glow. That seemed to have a calming effect on them, as if they had begun to realise, Duwara and Utongo alike, that some essential things would not change.

When the sunlight reached the rock on which the pups lay, they too became still. They turned their heads towards the new day, and their eyes, until now held tight shut, opened ever so slightly, just enough to give off a gleam of reflected light. Then they closed them again. This, for them, was a new day in a new world, and they would have to come into it gradually.

There was a sudden hush among one large group of meerkats. They were looking towards the nearest Deepden mound. They had noticed two meerkats on top of it. The silence spread as the other meerkats turned towards the mound and fell quiet.

The mound was some distance away, but the slightly bent figure could not be mistaken. It was Crossclaw. The much smaller meerkat with him was Fara.

Crossclaw was standing absolutely still. He might have been sculpted out of the hard sand on which he stood. His concentration on the sun was complete as it finally cleared the horizon and appeared in its full glory as an orb of molten gold. He straightened, stood a moment longer, then slowly lowered his body to the ground. He laid his head on his outstretched paws and was still.

Crossclaw had decided that he wanted to enjoy one more Sunwake, and see the Duwara sun one last time. He must have known, somewhere deep inside him, what news Tuft was going to bring back from his journey. He did not want to hear it, did not want to live under this new sky, where there would be fewer certainties; so he left.

Fara paused a moment, then she began to lick the motionless

old body. She did it gently and thoroughly; and from head to tail, as all the meerkats watched. Then when she had finished – yes, finished – she lay down alongside Crossclaw and waited. Her fur shone in the early light. The rest of the Duwara would no doubt join her soon.

Sheena left too, but in happier fashion than Crossclaw. She left atop Mpole's head. She could do nothing more here. The Utongo and the Duwara would have to work out their destiny together in this changed world they found themselves in. The two parts, no longer divided by The Gorge, would perhaps, perhaps, become a whole.

Her departure was hardly noticed, but she did not much mind that. She had her own life to return to.

Sandstepper and Pebble alone among the meerkats watched them leave. Pebble ran a little way after them as Mpole swayed off towards the slope that would take them down to the track leading to the campsite.

'Goodbye!' he called to Sheena.

'Enjoy your new world,' Sheena replied, 'but Beware the Black Hairy Thick-Tail!'

They passed close to the mound on which Crossclaw lay. Fara had stayed by his side. Perhaps she would soon be given a new name.

Chapter Thirty-Two: Jua

What always goes down
And always comes up,
The golden chalice
Where all may sup.

Sheena was sorry not to have seen Spickle again before she left.
There had been no sign of him or his parents at Rockhome. She
hoped they had not been harmed at all during the restlessness of
the day before. Either tribe could have chosen to regard
Nungunungu as treacherous.

Half-way down the slope, however, they caught up with two-
and-a-half spiky figures shambling alongside the grove of trees
where Sheena had first set eyes on Nyegere. They were just about
to head off at right-angles to the slope: a few minutes later and
they would have been out of sight.

Sheena urged Mpole close to them. 'They're friends,' she said.

When they reached the porcupines Mpole pointed his trunk at
them and sniffed loudly and suspiciously.

'Careful!' Sheena cautioned. The last thing she wanted was for
Mpole to vacuum up a bunch of quills. They would have burst
his bag, without doubt.

'We've had enough of agreements,' Nungu said by way of
explanation for their departure from Rockhome.

'From now on, it's just us Nungunungu.'

'From now on, it's just us Nungunungunungu,' said Spickle.

There was only one farewell left after that one. Sheena and Mpole talked a lot during the journey to the campsite, knowing that they might have only a short time together.

'Yes, I'm Accepted,' said Mpole, when Sheena asked him about what had happened after he had passed Mitihani Saba.

'But the tests haven't stopped. It seems that life itself is Mtihani Kubwa – One Big Test.'

Sheena could only agree.

Sheena was well hidden in the back of the Land Rover when, a few days later, it set off on the homeward journey. She had rather lost track of time while she was with the meerkats, and when she and Mpole reached Monkey Bluff Campsite she had found that the Allens' stay was coming to an end but wasn't quite there yet.

She had taken the opportunity to have one or two minor adventures with Mpole.

Very early on this last morning Mpole had helped her by creating a diversion while the Allens were packing the camping gear into the back of the Land Rover.

'Help! It's that elephant!' Mum Allen cried when he showed himself, with careful timing, at the far end of the clearing where they had camped. They had just about finished loading, and the Land Rover's rear doors were still open.

'It's that awful elephant that tried to trample Thomas!'

'It's that elephant that nearly trampled Annie!' cried Amy. She had left her favourite doll at home when they set off on this trip, because of what had nearly happened last time.

'It's the elephant that tried to stick its tusks into *Great White*'s radiator!' said Dad Allen.

Each one of them mis-remembered the events of the year before in his or her own way and according to what was most precious to them; and each one of them thought there was a very good reason for staying well clear of Mpole.

Only Thomas saw things in a different way and, utterly interested, he began to walk towards the young elephant.

Sheena had hoped they would all just panic and jump into the Land Rover, leaving the rear doors open for her. This was even better. The other three members of the family squawked, ran after Thomas, grabbed him by various bits and hauled him backwards to the Land Rover – Mum Allen by his trouser belt, Dad Allen by his ear, and Amy by a fold of loose skin behind his left knee, which she nipped painfully and gleefully.

By the time they got him back to *Great White*, Sheena was safely inside, out of sight among the tent bags, water containers (empty, now) and boxes. Dad Allen threw the remaining items in, slammed the rear doors, jumped into the driving seat. and drove off erratically through the trees and onto the track that would take them to the Park Gate.

Sheena, hidden by a folding table that had been leant up against the back of Thomas's and Amy's seat, was able to stretch up and look out of the rear window. Mpole was standing very still, watching the Land Rover depart. Then he lifted his trunk and trumpeted most impressively. Thomas reached over his father's shoulder most cheekily and beeped the Land Rover's horn in reply.

The sun had just come up over the higher ground to the East. It was perfectly round, perfectly bright, perfectly pure, perfectly everything.

'Take a good look!' said Dad Allen. 'This is the last time you'll see the Baragandiri sun!'

'Don't be silly, Daddy!' said Amy. 'It'll be the same sun when we get back home!'

'And what's so special about it anyway?' said Thomas, who was still disgruntled about being rescued from the elephant.

'It's only the sun.'

And...

...this is only one of (so far) three stories about Sheena's secret safaris to Baragandiri.

The previous two take place in The Main Park (look at the bottom right-hand corner of the map on Pages 2 and 3). If you haven't already read them, you may want to do so in order to learn more about Paka Mdogo, our little cat heroine...and about Mpole, the Gradual Elephant, and about baboons and lions and warthogs and vultures and vervet monkeys and another monitor lizard and two eagles and a python and a cobra and...

For more information go to http://www.ypdbooks.com or http://www.litworks.com/childrens.php, or ask at your local bookstore.